REKINDLED SPARKS

TALES OF MYTHON BOOK 3

KATHRYN JAYNE

Sometimes lightning strikes the same place twice.

PROLOGUE

There is no denying it. Hearing it is the year 224 can be quite confusing, especially if you don't know the real truth of history. But I am not talking B.C. or A.D. No, I am talking O.D. or Óla Dei, meaning 'all seen'. It's also, quite aptly, the abbreviation used for an overdose, which is something we all experienced a few hundred years ago, an overdose of the unseen. Our world forever changed, but you won't find that in your history books.

Before our year counter reset, your time ended, or at least it did for us. You continued on, unaware of what actually happened, and if my tales make it out of this region, then no doubt they will be passed over as fable, but this is our truth, this world is our truth.

As with most ends, it came as a complete force of devastation. The Doomsday clock leapt to midnight and the world as we knew it ended. But it wasn't missiles flying or chemicals assailing the sky, it was those who had existed unseen amongst us since the beginning, stepping into the light and making themselves known. These creatures, beings thought only to be spun from the minds of fablers like myself, had grown weary of living in the shadows, hiding their true nature, and Mankind fell to them in the blink of an eye and a new order was forced upon us.

But things changed too quickly, and the devastation was too great. That was when the Perennials came. Remember the story of how man obtained fire? Remember the gods of old? That was actually the Perennials. Invoking their powerful magics, these beings sacrificed themselves to rewrite history, turning back the clock for many minds and reaching into the great source of all to ensure no one your side would remember the truth.

They took it upon themselves to banish our land, remove it from sight and history, and seal within it as many of the creatures from your myths and legends as they could gather. Certain people in your history have worked alongside them, hunting these beings and directing their fate accordingly, sometimes relocating them to the island of Mython.

The problem is, Mython is a big island, and those of us here still have tales and books detailing the true history in all its horrific glory. Having seen how creatures had ravished the land, suffice to say our beginning was not an era of peace and harmony.

While the world outside had forgotten we had ever existed and moved into their new century, we eventually, through wars, rebellions and negotiations, found our own balance of sorts; one that is maintained by the most powerful of each race, those with Elder blood coursing through their veins.

Our country is divided into territories, each with its own elected leader who reports issues of note to the council, a collection of thirteen species predominately consisting of Elder bloodlines from the main preternatural lines such as shifter, fey, vampire, magical innate, elementals, celestials and so on. Humans were of course included, but we elect our own representatives just as any clan without such a sovereign did. The only missing faction is the Perennial, because none exist any more, at least none that we are aware of. After creating order, in our world and yours, it is said they invoked the last of their magic to seal our land from discovery.

Over two hundred years have passed since the wars died down and an uneasy truce was formed. The balance appears to be working. Now, life has returned to normal, or at least a manner of normal only possible here. Humans and preternatural are sharing space and resources, and the council are doing what is needed to maintain peace.

As I mentioned before, I am a fabler and it is my calling to tell the tales of our people. My name is Kathryn Jayne, and the tale here is just one of the many lives that call to me. Hopefully, what limited powers I have will guide it to your hands. Be it fiction in your eyes or not, these stories must be told.

CHAPTER 1

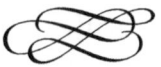

Maya's skin prickled. There it was again, that feeling of being watched, of someone's eyes upon her. She had felt it for days now, an electricity in the air that sent shivers chasing across her flesh. She shoved her hands deep into her grey princess coat's pockets, her fingers wrapping around her key-chain, caressing the panic alarm as she quickened her pace.

It was only a five-minute walk from where she'd parked her car, but seeing the ambulance depot in the distance brought little comfort. Sinister occurrences had no distance gauge. She was grateful that, despite it being autumn, the dark nights had yet to fully encroach, at least with the twilight sky above, the shadows weren't as dark and menacing.

She was always more apprehensive this time of year. Three years ago today her best friend, Raiden, had vanished without a trace. Their parting had left her hollow, as if a piece of her had vanished along with him. The worst part was, as far as anyone else was concerned, he'd never even existed.

She still recalled the way he had kissed her that night, stealing her breath as his lips met hers in a flurry of desperation, lust, and sadness. He had pulled away, his ice-blue eyes glistening with unshed tears as he studied her every contour with an oppressive weight that had terrified her. Something about how he had looked at her had seemed so final. He'd lingered at her door, weaving his hands within her long, dark brown hair, muttering an apology as he pressed his forehead to hers.

The next thing she knew she was waking in bed nursing a migraine, and Raiden was nowhere to be found. As the days rolled on, she began to worry. His device was disconnected— which happened more often than she'd like given his line of work—but more troubling was that no one but her seemed to remember him. Not her work friends, not her neighbours, not even her best friend, Carley.

He hadn't just vanished from her life; he'd faded from existence. Just weeks before he disappeared, she had completed her surgical residency and so, she used her increased access to search the hospital records, remembering how her father had treated him for multiple stab wounds not long after they had met. But it was as if he had never existed, as if their friendship, their relationship, had been nothing more than a figment of her imagination.

With Raiden's sudden disappearance and her father's death just the week before, it had all been too much. She had driven herself to the brink of madness trying to find him. At first, it gave her something else to think about rather than focusing on her father's death. She'd known in her heart the only reason he'd hung on as long as he had was so he could be there the day she qualified. Perhaps this loss was the reason finding Raiden had consumed her, why she had never been able to let him go. But she knew it was more than that, more than obsession. She had loved him so fiercely that, without him, she'd lost herself.

Her work friends had grown concerned, talking in hushed tones of a mental breakdown, using the fact her father had died as its cause. She had ignored their whispers for almost twelve months, twelve months of sidelong glances and veiled whispers, before taking the bridge course and changing professions, from surgeon to medic.

Her move had surprised them; while personally, she had been a mess, her skill as a surgeon never wavered. Her real motives were kept guarded. She knew better than to tell anyone that the reason for this move was to allow her access to chip location data, but she soon discovered it was impossible to find someone who didn't exist in any place but her memories.

For her, turning her back on a career she loved, hoping to find the person who had been her everything, had been the most natural thing in the world. But it had been three years now, and aside from the occasional phantom scent that caused her to scan the faces of those around, she'd found nothing to prove he had ever existed. Almost nothing.

Those at work, even her best friend, Carley, had thought her imaginary boyfriend was harmless, a coping mechanism, believing that her overwhelmed mind created a man in her life to replace the one she had lost.

She had been close to her father. Even with

his busy schedule, he had always been present and attentive. He had been this hospital's lead trauma surgeon, and their shared passion had been one of the reasons she had chosen the medical profession. She had mourned his loss, even lost herself to grief for a short time, but no matter what anyone said, she knew Raiden was real. If she needed proof, if ever she faltered or thought she should give up and believe their lies, then she only had to dig a little deeper into her pocket for her fingers to touch the small graphite stone he'd given her on their third date.

He'd vowed to one day upgrade it to a diamond, but had said, like graphite, relationships first needed to survive heat and pressure to be forged into something magnificent. It had been the most romantic thing she had ever heard. After just three dates they had known they were it for each other, although she had only needed one. She had known the moment her almost black eyes had met his stark, contrasting ice-blue ones that he was the end. There could be no other.

She had paid to get the stone mounted onto a setting and fixed to the silver bracelet that used to belong to her mother, but between night shifts, studying, and wanting to drink in his presence every spare minute she could, it had taken her so long to get around to having it done that he'd never had the chance to see it.

The only time it ever came off was when she dressed for work or went out dancing, but still, she carried it, keeping it close, always in her possession. If not for this memento she may have agreed with Carley, with the catty whispers that had followed her outside the theatres, and consider that she had indeed lost herself indulging in flights of fancy.

Sometimes it was easier to believe a lie than fight for the truth.

Who was to say she hadn't just found a rock and invented the story? Digging her hands deeper into her pocket, she shook her head, knowing better than to flirt with insecurities. She had tried to move on with her life, but her heart would never let her forget. His every detail, from his hair coloured like storms and starlight to the way the crisp scent of fresh winter snow surrounded him, was forever burned in her mind and heart.

Even though the chip-tracking data had proven a dead end, she never considered returning to surgery. In an ambulance at least she could look for him on the streets during their patrol, instead of hoping he'd turn up in hospital. She glanced over her shoulder, the prickling sensation of being watched was still present even as the soft ambient light from outside the depot washed over her.

Placing the back of her wrist against the sensor, she waited for her chip credentials to register. It took barely a breath before the doors swept open and she was inside, away from the prickling heat of the unwanted watcher's stare. She glanced back over her shoulder as the door closed, wondering if she would catch sight of them. Within a moment, all she could see was her own intensely dark brown eyes staring back at her.

The siren wailed. Its shrieking cry ordered people aside as the ambulance careened down the city streets, weaving in and out of cars and skirting around barriers on the wrong side of the road as it tore its path through the city. Blue strobes illuminated the air, casting a vibrant hue against the darkening sky, bathing clubbers and party-goers with a brief taste of things to come once they were granted entry into their chosen establishment.

Maya's fingers curled tighter around the fold-down seat, its coarse fabric yielding to her touch as she held on for dear life. She was thrown from side to side, her long ponytail whipping around with each hastily taken corner. The world sped past her through the small window in a blur, but she knew better now than to watch it flash by.

Her vision remained fixed on the loaded tranquiliser gun, clipped into place on her left. The rattling of the clasps set her nerves on edge as it fought to make a daring escape. She didn't trust the holdings, even with their fingerprint activated release. They had failed once before with embarrassing consequences, one of which was her unfortunate nickname, Bambi. It didn't matter how many times she had protested that it was his mother who was shot, her dark brown hair and large brown eyes had sealed her fate.

"One minute to ETA," Mike called through the small open partition which doubled as a door separating the driver from the cabin. This blond-haired man was the one responsible for her perpetual motion sickness. He was an excellent driver—his skills were formidable—and Maya had no doubt he could conquer the racetrack circuits with ease and hold his own against any professional in the world beyond the barrier, while barely breaking a sweat.

She, however, already felt the waves of heat washing over her and was grateful she always skipped breakfast when was rotated with the Stig. He was known for his record response time for a reason. He exploited every opportunity and read the roads and his surroundings with the same ease as breathing. If ever she needed help— or even a getaway driver—she could only hope he would be the person behind the wheel.

Peeling one of her hands from the safety of the seat, she reached beneath, her fingers sliding around the smooth, braided handle of her personal equipment. Each medic had their own bag and was responsible for the items within, but given Maya's dual qualifications, she had access to far more tools than the average medic. This single large bag contained almost everything she could possibly need for whatever emergency they approached. Except for the tranquiliser gun. She would have felt a lot better if that piece of kit was accompanying them inside. She ran a finger across the hidden hook-and-loop sealed pocket she'd added to her belt, confirming the small tranquiliser dart was still secure in its holding.

After the transfer, she had soon discovered medics were not as respected as they should be. She had never realised how much abuse they suffered for just trying to help. Whilst the same could be said of many medical professions, this one seemed to carry more risk. Unlike in the hospitals where the patients were made to wear a suppressor and had all possessions removed on admittance, out here, the patients still had access to weaponry and their latent abilities.

Just eight months ago, someone had tried to hold her hostage, hoping to trade her life for the medicines they carried. Luckily she was already carrying the dart on her by then since just a week before another patient had tried to stab her, not to mention the time when the newly turned vampire had thought to call them as if they were a meals-on-wheels service. Being a medic was not safe, although it made for some entertaining stories.

She had been in her fair share of scenarios where the dart she concealed on her person had come in handy. The gun, however, was for the more dangerous situations, such as berserkers. If the notification they received was accurate, this would be just a run-of-the-mill resuscitation. But that meant nothing these days.

Even with the reports of violence and altercations, they were expected to go out without issued stab vests or defensive tools. Despite the number of attacks that occurred, the public only ever heard about a very select few; the rest were swept away, logged but ignored, meaning the underlying issues were never addressed.

Over the last year, things had become worse, to the point her Station Officer had purchased protective clothing for his teams from his own pocket, and many other depots across Mython had followed suit. The only times they wore official body armour was when summoned into dangerous situations with the Blue Coats, all other times the public expected to see the golden Rod of Asclepius displayed on the front and back of their green uniform. Maya gave her shirt a tug. She still wasn't convinced the thin vest she wore under it could stop a knife, but apparently, it was the leading edge in discrete protection.

She ran through a mental checklist, her small ritual as she unfastened the belt. While Mike was known for his impressive driving skill, she too had notability. No one tried harder to prevent someone from dying. She went above and beyond, utilised every resource, and fought beyond the window to call time of death for the chance of one more breath. Everyone fought for this, but her success rate of dragging someone back from the underworld was impressive, so much so that Station Officer Silvers had scheduled her for an aptitude test, convinced the unidentified Magic Innate—MI—coding of her blood would prove her to be a healer, despite her earlier testing as a child showing no affinity.

At birth, everyone had their blood registered into type and coding. The coding fell into several categories: EB, meaning the person possessed elder blood, beings believed to have descended from a mortal and divinity pairing, adding extra power to their hereditary talents; MI—Magic Innate, suggesting the person has preternatural tendencies towards manipulating energy and magic or someone in their family once possessed a gift; and NM—Neutral Mundane or Non-Magical, which applied to a majority of the human population.

There were other classes that identified clans; for instance, vampires were categorised as HC, belonging to the Hematophagy Clan since they consumed blood; and shifters were MC, part of the Metamorphic Clan, as they possessed the ability to alter shape. The lists went on, but categorisation meant a medic at least knew what to expect when their device connected to the biometric chip that a large majority of Mython possessed.

These chips were nothing short of amazing. They not only tracked a person's health and location, but allowed them to pay for goods and services, or even access their home computer files from any device. The chips also allowed people access to secure buildings, like the ambulance station and even many homes these days, so long as they had the correct credentials. If it was electronic, this chip could regulate it and thus made the need to carry anything else redundant.

The sirens silenced, bringing her back from thoughts. That was her cue to move. As her hand rested on the rear doors, she took one final glance towards the tranquiliser gun before disembarking.

The setting sun had just started to dip below the horizon, teasing the solar-charged streetlights into life. Curtains twitched as nosey neighbours peered outside, their inside lights betraying their curiosity as the beams escaping from parted curtains illuminated manicured and overgrown gardens alike.

At the end of the short, cracked driveway, light spilt from the open door causing the few weeds growing between time-worn cracks to cast long shadows down the narrow winding path that led to her destination. Shadowed by the light, the silhouette of a young girl stood waving desperately, her teddy bear gripped tightly by its paw as she jumped up and down shouting through tears that her daddy was in here.

Maya's feet struck the uneven paving, her

heavy boots making her run sound like thunder as she hurried up the path, past the young girl in rainbow pyjamas, and into the house, knowing Mike would be on her heels after securing the vehicle.

From the second she crossed the threshold, she was assailed by family photographs. Frames lined the wall, some purchased, others clearly crafted with love from wood, pasta, and glitter. She didn't stare, she barely passed her gaze over them, but she saw so many natural, unposed pictures of happy times and treasured moments covering almost every free space in the narrow hall.

Glancing upstairs towards the bedrooms she paused, her instincts told her whoever needed aid was downstairs. Her gaze lingered on the far door at the end of the hall. Given the uniform layout of most houses, it was probably the kitchen, just as she knew, as she stepped through the left door, she would find herself in the living room.

Light spilt through the slender bell light-shade of the high ceiling, causing the glass remains of the small coffee table to glisten, almost creating a halo around the muscular man's frame. Like his family, he was in his pyjamas, the ebony black fabric making his pallor look even more cadaverous. Darker staining on the carpet wafted the familiar odour of coffee.

Maya inhaled again, catching small remnants of the pizza and chips they must have had for tea and the undertones of popcorn that originated from a small bowl at the side of the worn three-seater sofa. A tiny blonde woman leaned over her husband's enormous frame, her dainty hands pushing at him, silently begging him to wake as tears traced her soft jawline.

"Ma'am, can you tell me what happened here?" Maya questioned, placing her finger to the man's throat. Nothing. The woman glanced up, her lips moving soundlessly. "Was he complaining of any pain, has he taken something, eaten anything unusual?" she questioned, her fingers sliding across her device until it chirped, notifying her the man's chip had synced with her device. A quick glance at the screen showed the black-haired subject, one Fredrick McArther, classified as NM, Normal Mundane. Flat-lined for three minutes and counting.

She had just finished her assessment and started chest compressions when she heard the front door close as Mike walked in, behind her by only half a minute. With a confirmatory nod to Maya, he placed his arm on the grieving woman, escorting her further away, trying to pry some further information from her that might be of aid. Mike could always coax information from even the most terrified or grieving witness. Despite his dare-devil driving, he had an air of warmth about him. If she was viewed as the little sister of the station, he was the father.

Sweat formed on Maya's brow as she began a new cycle, her knee burning from the shards of glass grinding beneath her. Mike would no doubt pull her up on the fact she'd not put her knee pads in, again. She leaned down, breathing for him, watching his chest rise and fall as she forced oxygen into his lungs.

"Come on, beat," she whispered, her eyes drawn to the stricken girl who now stood watching as Maya began her next cycle of compressions. The young girl shared her father's dark hair. She stood by the fireplace, her heartbroken face a sheer contrast to the many photographs behind her. "Beat," Maya whispered in time with each compression.

She breathed for him again. Another cycle, another near-silent prayer as heat and electricity began to chase through her. Then she heard it. The faint bleeping from her device to say there was a pulse. Placing her ear to the man's mouth, she waited, looking down at his chest, hoping to see it rise, or feel the hint of a breath upon her skin. Sweat trickled down her spine, tingling like electricity as it traced its path, and the silence stretched on. Nothing.

She breathed for him, her mantra altering. "Breathe," she whispered. A smile tickled her lips as she leaned back, his chest rising as he pulled in a breath. She could see Mike hovering at the adjoining door and gave him a slight nod. "Good man. Now, let me take another look at you." Maya began her secondary examination, noticing just a few minor cuts and scrapes caused by the shattered glass. "You're looking good. If you would just wake up for me." She continued to talk softly. "That's it, open your eyes," she coaxed as his eyelids began to flutter. After her first month on the job, Maya had found talking softly, telling people what was needed from them, always seemed to help.

The man's brown eyes opened, meeting Maya's vacantly. "Now, sir, can you tell me your name?"

Pulling his hood down further with a sharp tug to ensure his face was shielded from anyone who happened to catch a glimpse of him, Blaze watched through the open crack of the curtains as Maya Jarrett assessed the patient with ease. Her every movement was measured with no energy lost through needless motions, something no doubt learnt from her long hours in surgery.

The indoor lighting caused the sweat on her skin to glisten as she pushed down on the man's chest, her ponytail cascaded over her shoulders, nestling upon her bare skin, brushing against her cleavage in a way that made his fingers, and parts of him he didn't dare acknowledge, ache with the need to touch her. A seductress, that was what she was. Every rise of her chest, each flick of her hair, called to him while the fierce passion in her eyes made him shudder.

She was not a person to back down or to be overwhelmed by odds stacked against her, in work anyway. He had seen the way her boyfriend treated her; the only thing that man hadn't done was literally wipe his feet on her as he took advantage of her generosity. In work, she was a force to be reckoned with. In her personal life, however, she lost that confidence. The only time he saw it emerge again was when she and Carley went dancing.

He knew he shouldn't be watching her so closely, being seen could jeopardise everything, but she was his addiction and flirting with a danger she could not possibly understand. He felt the charge chase across his flesh as the man's heart began to beat. Another name for his list, another person brought back from the dead. He had hoped after his first warning—after he started the pyres—she would have understood, that she would have stopped playing god.

He made a note on his device before slipping away into the shadows. She had an alibi; for the next half an hour, she would be completing assessments and investigations to determine if Fredrick McArther could remain home or required a trip to the hospital for a follow-up. Which meant now was the perfect time to act.

Slinking away, he started his bike, his device already tracking his next target. He had plenty of time to neutralise her and send a warning. Something a little more direct. He had killed thirteen people in her name so far. He had started subtly, but she wasn't learning her lesson. He had needed to go bigger, get recognised, and even with his deeds reaching the news, still she hadn't realised what he was doing for her. It was about time Maya Jarrett realised that she was the reason this was happening.

CHAPTER 2

*M*aya stifled a yawn as she sank into the cushion on the collapsible seat, her belt securing with a satisfying click. She was exhausted. Maybe Station Office Silvers was correct, maybe she did have a gift. Why else would bringing people back from the brink of death exhaust her?

After reorganising her bag and completing the necessary requisitions form to confirm supplies used, she unzipped the side pocket, pulling out an energy bar, tearing the wrapper with her teeth as the engine roared to life. Without the lights and sirens to cheer him on Mike's driving calmed, became almost normal.

"Well, Bambi, you've done it again," he called

back between the open partition door. "I know one little girl who'll be glad her daddy is sleeping at home tonight."

Medics in Mython were literally a trauma unit on wheels. Their role was to treat and stabilise a patient on-site, only transferring them to a medical facility if their condition warranted more severe or long-term intervention. They dealt with everything from stitches to emergency x-rays at the patient's home thanks to the specialist equipment that synchronised with their devices.

Fortunately, after his brush with death, Fredrick McArther passed the physical and mental assessments with ease, and the system flagged him as safe to remain at home, and so, he was able to stay with his family. A nurse would stop by on her rounds in the morning to check on him. "So, when is your affinity testing?" he pried. She knew Mike preferred it when she sat up front beside him, but his driving was far more terrifying when she could see the headlights of other vehicles racing towards her.

"In the morning, our S.O. arranged it for when I get off shift so I don't have to come back. I don't see the point though, I've already tested negative," she answered around a mouthful of her energy bar. Now the race was over she was more than happy to eat. If she didn't, it was unlikely she'd make it through the shift. She grimaced looking at the paper wrapping, realising it was one of Rick's. He brought these cheap and nasty things, then ate all of hers and thought it balanced out. She supposed she should be grateful he brought anything at all; normally he didn't bother. In fact, she was certain he'd only picked these up because she'd pulled him up on it when she'd been left with no food in the house to take to work.

"To be honest, I'm surprised he didn't do it sooner. Anyone MI gets a test on starting to work for us."

"Yeah, they assumed I'd had it done during my residency, but firstly my paperwork went missing, then whenever it was scheduled I always ended up in a long surgery, then with my father's death and... well, I ended up doing the bridge course before a date was set.

"To be honest, I think initially my father had something to do with the interference. He saw how devastated I was when I was little. Not only did I find out I wasn't in my father's clan due to some strange genetic anomaly, but I didn't even have a gift that made it worth the trade. You try telling a seven-year-old that it was nothing to be upset about."

"Want your usual?" It was only as he asked Maya realised he'd already pulled into the twenty-four-hour drive-through. Glancing at her fob watch, she nodded to herself. Their shift had only just begun. She was going to need more than a few injections of coffee if the night continued at its current pace.

"You need to ask, it's my turn, isn't it?" Mike leaned through the window, presenting his wrist to the reader to complete payment before Maya had time to unclip her belt. With a shake of her head, she walked into the cab through the partition to sit beside him.

A few moments later, they were parked, enjoying their hot drink and freshly made sandwiches.

"So, Bambi, you nervous about the testing?"

Looking towards him, she smiled, folding her empty sandwich wrappers into a small square on her lap. "Not really, as I said, I was tested at seven, there's really nothing special about me. How's Daisy and the baby?"

"They're doing well, Christian is sleeping through now, which helps. Daisy keeps telling me now he's sleeping better I can pick up some extra shifts again if I want, but to be honest, I've liked being able to do the nights so she can rest. I can straighten the place up, you know, take some

of the pressure off. I don't want her burning out."
As he spoke, he showed her the latest
photographs on his device. Each time Maya
looked at the little bundle, she couldn't help but
notice how much he had grown.

"You're a softy." She smiled, cooing over the
photographs.

"Only where family's concerned." He
grinned. Maya smiled back before savouring a
sip of her drink. Despite his aggressive driving,
Mike was one of the kindest people she knew.
Before she'd accidentally let it slip that his
driving could put the Stig to shame, his
nickname had reflected his good nature. She
loved watching old shows from beyond the
barrier, and since a lot of her co-workers were
male, they had a good idea about what program
she was referring to, and the name had stuck to
him like Bambi had to her.

Her transition two years ago had been a lot
smoother than she had anticipated. She hadn't
been deaf to the rumours that circulated thanks
to a rather vindictive nurse whose advances she
had refused several times. Here, however,
everyone seemed to think of her as their little
sister. Even those younger than her seemed
somehow protective towards her, possibly
because she was the only woman on their male-

dominated night-shift team. "So you seeing your fellow after work?"

"Hmm." Maya took a sip of her drink, trying to pretend the mention of Rick hadn't made the coffee taste just a little bitter.

"Trouble in paradise?"

"He wants me to change to days to fit in with his shifts." That wasn't Rick's only problem. She worked a four-on-four-off shift rota. Normally he didn't give a damn about aligning their off-days, but suddenly, since she'd agreed to cover Davey's shifts while he dealt with a family emergency, it was his new line of complaint.

She was coming close to the end of a twenty-eight-day stretch and, apparently, because she didn't want to stay awake on his days off, she was being selfish. The problem with nights was they worked on a small crew, so cover was difficult to come by. With Mike job-sharing and only having two crews in operation at night, it meant cover had to come from either day staff or the other night shift. Maya was always glad to pick up the extra hours, and not just because it gave her a break from Rick's moaning; she still hadn't given up her search. Each extra hour on shift was another chance to find him.

"And?"

"And nothing, I want to work nights, he

knew that getting in. I already get up early to pick him up from work most days, but he isn't willing to compromise and stay up late when he's off. Apparently, I'm selfish, wanting to keep my body clock on night shift hours when I'm off. I don't ask him to stay up with me, but that doesn't stop him finding the energy to suddenly stay out until three to go drinking with his mates. Or complaining when I have the audacity to arrange a night out with Carley. Honestly, what do you men want?" She huffed out a sharp breath, lifting the loose strands that had escaped her ponytail away from her face.

"On behalf of the male species, I apologise." Mike held his hands up in surrender, a smile tugging at his lips.

"Honestly, Mike, I've already had to have words with him about trying to move in. Just last week I caught him bringing boxes of his things over while I was out. I don't mind him staying the odd night, but according to Carley he's been spending his nights at mine playing games with his friends while I'm working and I'm footing the utility bills." She left out the way he left the house in shambles, how he never cleaned up after himself but had the audacity to moan if she hadn't made the time to clean up. Or how he emptied her cupboards and treated her more like a waitress than a girlfriend when his friends came over.

"How long have you been together now?" Mike asked, taking the final sip from his mug, he tossed it through the window into one of the recycling units, pumping his arm playfully as he sunk it effortlessly.

"Six months."

"Do you like him?" The way he looked at her suggested he knew the truth, that he could see through the lies she told herself.

"He's nice enough when he's not blatantly taking advantage. It's just he's not—" She glanced to her hands in her lap. *He's not Raiden,* she finished quietly to herself. For three years, he had been missing, and no one in all that time had made her feel the way he had. Not even close. She gave a sigh, wondering what could have happened to him.

They had been happy, they had fit seamlessly into one another's lives like the missing pieces of a puzzle right until the day he'd vanished. Mike reached over, squeezing her arm, showing her she had worn her sadness a little too openly. "So, tell me more about Christian." She saw the sparkle in Mike's eyes return as he began to tell her all the new things his adorable baby boy was doing.

~

Maya sat in the small office's waiting room looking at the plain carpets. Her unblinking gaze formed all manner of three-dimensional shapes from the uneven shag until she was convinced the carpet was moving, or something within it was. She blinked several times, each time resetting the room back to its original state, only for the tired distortion to begin again.

The carpet was starting to make her eyes burn, but it still took a great effort to pull her gaze up to the eggshell-coloured walls to the constantly cycling, digital health posters that had sprung to life the moment she entered. She glanced to the glass-panelled office door, seeing only her tired reflection looking back, and quickly averted her gaze before she had time to think about how exhausted she looked.

Leaning back into the chair, she closed her eyes, grateful the appraiser had agreed to meet her at the hospital. Typically, adults being tested had to travel to their offices, which not only would have meant a long drive but a longer wait. The appointment had been scheduled months ago, long before she knew she'd be on such a long stretch. She had to remember to thank Station Officer Silvers. He was bound to have pulled some strings to arrange for the examiner to not only come here but to see her before their normal working hours.

"Miss Jarrett." The voice startled her. Opening her eyes, she found herself looking at the office door where a homely woman stood waiting, her warm smile instantly putting Maya's tired nerves at ease. She was dressed in casual trousers with a pale brown shirt that was almost the exact colour of her bobbed hair. She hadn't realised anyone had been in there and was instantly concerned that she should have knocked to announce her presence, rather than just taking a seat. "Thank you for coming. This won't take long. I trust you are familiar with the process?" Maya nodded, stepping past as the examiner held the sliding door open. "Very well, take a seat, and we shall begin."

The released door slid back into place with a whisper-soft sigh, sealing them within the small office. It was of simple design, a small wooden desk, three chairs and a monitor. Next to the desk, currently covered in all manner of rods, cylinders, and spheres, was an old-fashioned doctor's bag, its yawning mouth open, revealing its suede interior to be empty.

For the next hour the appraiser, who Maya came to learn was called Emily Clarkson, proceeded to pass her various items crafted from crystal and metal with the instruction to close her eyes and hold on to them until told otherwise.

One by one, they made their way through Emily's assorted rods, spheres, and cones. The only time she felt even the slightest sensation was when the rod containing graphite was placed within her grasp. It was minimal, nothing more than a sensation of warmth. When the test was over, Emily glanced down at the notes in her digital notebook based on visible reactions and the data collected from Maya's chip.

"Well, Miss Jarrett, given your responses, it appears you have no active affinities. The graphite is the only item to which you had a mild reaction. Unfortunately, your reaction to the stimulus was far below any response required in order to make further testing worthwhile." Emily glanced up as she collected the remaining artifacts from the small pine desk between them to slip them into her bag before snapping the hinged opening closed.

"I appreciate you coming out for the testing, sorry to have wasted your time."

"Oh no, Miss Jarrett, this wasn't a waste of time. I'm happy to help." The way her smile reached her eyes put Maya at ease. "Now, that's everything I need. Thanks for making time for me after your shift. I'll deliver the results to Station Officer Silvers personally when I've just checked over a few things." The way a slight blush crept into her cheeks made Maya think this woman had an entirely different motive to seeing her S.O. than delivering the report.

"Thank you."

Maya didn't remember driving home. One minute she was walking to her car, the next she was pulling up the drive to stop in front of her house wondering how she got there. She had just finished her twenty-seventh night, having picked up extra shifts to cover for Davey. One more night and she was back to her normal four-on-four-off, and she was really looking forward to the rest. She had plans with the sofa, a tub of her favourite ice cream, the television and, if the stars aligned, maybe a night out with Carley. It had been too long since they last went dancing, and she could feel the tension creeping across her shoulders begging for release.

As she stepped through her deep-red front door, she groaned. Ridges of dried mud marred her otherwise spotless wooden flooring, flooring she had spent an hour cleaning before leaving for work last night after Rick had left his spilt soda trailing across the floor. By the time she had got up, the fluids had set into a sticky treacly mess, leaving her no choice but to clean it or risk being inundated with pests.

Slipping her shoes off and placing them on the small rack to the left of the door, she toyed with the idea of cleaning the dried flakes before slipping into bed. A quick glance at her watch told her it could wait. Rubbing the back of her neck, she made her way through the large lounge using the first of two doors that entered the kitchen. A tired smile eased a fraction of the tension as she saw the sandwich left on the side for her wrapped in beeswax.

Maybe Rick wasn't so bad after all. He'd left a mess, again, condiments and crumbs were scattered across the work surface, but at least he'd been thoughtful enough to make tea for her. She couldn't remember the last time he had been this thoughtful. Perhaps their last talk had an effect after all. Sitting at the small breakfast bar, she peeled away the paper, rinsing it ready for reuse and sat to enjoy her sandwich.

She was halfway through when she saw the manila envelope on the counter. Sliding it towards her, she slid her finger beneath the flap. Inside were two small pieces of paper. Tipping them onto the unit, she frowned, taking another bite of the sandwich. Looking back at her were two pictures, both of women with a red marker pen line over their faces and the word "STOP" scrawled over the background.

Grabbing the envelope, she turned it over: blank. She slid the pictures back inside. Clearly someone had pushed it through the wrong letterbox.

As she finished her sandwich, she let her imagination run away with her, wondering which of her neighbours this was intended for. She didn't really know them by name, but it was still a fun distraction to guess which husband had been caught having an affair—multiple affairs, she corrected. Her money was on the personal trainer-slash-dog walker, two doors down. She'd noticed his wandering eye several times. The question was, were these photos intended as a warning, or would a blackmail demand be the next thing to slip through her letterbox.

Her stomach churned as she peered back inside at the pictures. There was something familiar about one of the women. She must have seen her around the neighbourhood, so it looked like whoever was guilty wasn't straying too far from their home ground. Pushing her plate aside, she opened her device, messaging Rick.

Maya: Thanks for the sandwich. Where did you find the envelope?

Rick: That was my lunch, I was popping back for it. Can you make another and drop it at the front desk? The envelope was on the doormat this morning. Where else would it be?

She didn't miss the implication he had slept over at hers without asking. Again.

Maya: I've just got home, can you not pick one up from the deli?

Rick: Why should I have to spend my hard-earned money on something you could slap together in a matter of minutes? I was going to stop by for it on my break.

Maya: Fine. I'll drop one over.

Rick: Great. Your fridge is a little empty,

you also need milk and bread. Lunch is at twelve, so any time before then is great.

"You have got to be kidding me," she growled to no one in particular as she opened the fridge door. She had stocked it just two days ago. Now the only thing hogging the small spotlight that greeted her was a limp piece of kale sharing centre stage with a single stick of celery, complete with savage-looking teeth marks marring its outer edge. In the door was an empty bottle of milk, and next to it, another glass bottle with small amounts of residue from the fresh orange juice the milkman delivered that morning.

Muttering a curse, she snatched her coat from its hook and headed towards the store. Rick would have to cope with a pre-made sandwich, going out once was more than enough. If he thought she'd come home, make him another sandwich and head out again, he had another think coming. Really, would it kill him to replace the things he ate once in a while?

CHAPTER 3

A loud banging startled her from sleep. Grabbing her device, Maya saw it was a little after four o'clock, not the half-six she had intended after not getting home until just after noon. The next thing her tired eyes registered was over twenty missed calls and numerous unread messages. Her head pounded in time with each bang of the door. Even from upstairs, she could hear the cracking of the wood against the strain.

Fighting back the frost-white comforter, she reached under her bed to grab the baseball bat she had kept there since she was a little girl. Her father had given it to her when he started to have emergency patients dropping by the house at ungodly hours, day and night, the same time he had put a lock on her door instructing her to keep it locked at all times. This bedroom had always been her sanctuary and was one of two places Rick had no access to. Tiptoeing downstairs, she saw a hand reaching through, grappling with the chain before banging on the door again.

"May!" His growling voice saw her freeze on the bottom step, but knowing it was Rick outside didn't dispel her anxiety at expecting a burglar. It just morphed it into something else, anger. He knew if the chain was on she needed sleep. Lowering the bat, she made her way to the door. "About time. You put the chain on. Did you forget the guys were coming over?" Closing the door she attempted to breathe through her frustration as she released the chain.

She glanced over Rick's shoulder to see his two closest friends, Rob and Earl. She offered the two men a tired smile. They were both still dressed in their suits, almost making them appear like a security detail for the casually dressed blond man. Rick's fair hair was what first drew her attention. She knew it was from a bottle, that his blue eyes were contacts, but the platinum shade made it possible to almost imagine he was Raiden the night they met on the dance floor, and if she unfocused her eyes, and ignored the fact Rick's features were nowhere near as pleasing as Raiden's, she could almost pretend.

At first, she kept him around for nostalgia, a shadow of a person he could never be, a person it seemed she could never have, and she let him stay because she realised how much she missed companionship. She was settling, and she knew it. He probably would have known it too if he'd paid attention to anything other than her bank balance and breasts.

She thought she could make it work, learn to be fond of him—just fond because after Raiden there could be no other love—but after six months of effort on her part, she was beginning to realise there was not one part of her she could fool, not one piece of her that could stand the thought of a future with anyone that wasn't Raiden.

"Rick, I told you, I'm working tonight."

"That's alright, you stocked the fridge, didn't you? You can whip us up something to eat before you leave." At least his friends had the decency to look embarrassed. The truth was she knew she shouldn't let him treat her like this, but her guilt let him get away with it. Most of the time. She'd even turned a blind eye to the smell of unfamiliar perfume in their room. Their room, not the one she slept in when he wasn't here; only one man had a place there.

She and Rick shared a different bed, so not to sully the memories. This divide, this shadow Rick lived in, was why she allowed him to treat her as he did. It was why she felt guilty because even if Rick had put in the same effort she had, he could never hold a candle to Raiden. Being with him was unfair, to both of them, so in her own way, she thought she deserved him to treat her like this. She hadn't been leading him on, but she had known from the beginning any man could only be second best.

"That's okay, Rick. We can order pizza." Maya gave a grateful smile at Rob for his offer. He ran an embarrassed hand through his mahogany-brown hair. "Better yet, we can head back to my place this evening, let Maya have some quiet before her shift. How's work, you still on that stretch?" Her smile broadened, earning a frown from Rick, whose hand wrapped around her arm possessively, his short nails digging into her flesh a little too firmly.

Rob was normally rather quiet compared to the other two in the group. He was also the only one who ever seemed to help clear up after they'd crashed at her place, which lately seemed to be a frequent occurrence. This home had been in her family for a long time, with five bedrooms upstairs and large rooms downstairs. Rick was always telling her space to spare was space to share.

"Yes, tonight's my—"

"Nonsense, you don't mind, do you, May. It'll only take you half an hour or so. Doesn't take much to heat the oven and throw some food in."

"Actually, you know what?" Rob nudged Earl, the dark-haired, lanky figure to his right whose attention was fixed on his device, probably in an attempt to ignore the awkward conversation. "I just remembered, we were meant to meet Raj. I bet he'll be wondering where we are. You coming with us, Rick?" Maya saw Earl's fingers start to skim across his screen, no doubt setting up said meeting.

While Rick could be an inconsiderate arse, his friends always seemed to know when he was pushing the boundaries a little too far and often intervened. She wondered how he had friends who were so opposite to his own abrasive personality, or maybe it was just her he treated this way. He was, after all, more than happy to go out of his way for them. In fact, she didn't recall a harsh word towards them ever passing his lips.

"Give me a minute," he growled, pulling

Maya inside, pushing the door closed with his foot. "Well, thanks for that. Couldn't just throw a pizza in the oven, could you? You just had to cause a scene. Could you have been any less hospitable? You just humiliated me in front of my friends."

"Excuse me?" Enough was enough. She'd accepted more than her share of his crap out of her misguided notions of guilt, but this was her home, and right now she was too tired for his bullshit. Her recent racing thoughts put many things into perspective, and she realised exactly how much she let him get away with. Seriously, who let their apparent boyfriend bring another woman home and didn't pull him up on it, especially when finding their slinky lingerie wrapped in the unmade sheets of the bed.

Perhaps those photos had been meant for this house after all.

Maybe it was her fatigue, the mud still tracked across the floor, the morning spent restocking the food, or the way his nails dug into her flesh in that warning manner when she dared to smile at Rob, but somewhere amongst these things had been the final straw. In fact, the final straw should have been months ago.

"You heard."

"Get out." These two words left her lips like a

bullet, taking with them all the tension and weight of having him in her life. She breathed deeply, wondering when had been the last time that her chest expanded so fully with a breath. Now she was just angry, angry for letting him treat her the way he had. Even if she knew she had been settling, at least she had been trying.

"What?"

"You heard me, get out. This is *my* house, not your party den, not your free pantry or brothel. I don't expect to come home from work to find the place covered in mud and my cupboards bare, or some woman's underpants in my bed." She saw him blanch at that, but his reaction didn't stop her, it just fuelled her frustrations. "I spent all morning running around after you and dropping your food off, and you don't even have the decency to think I may need to sleep. I put the chain on, Rick, that should have told you I didn't want to be disturbed, but you just couldn't take a hint." She took a deep breath, fighting back the heat behind her eyes that warned her tears were on the way. Tears he would misinterpret.

"Well, if you weren't working all the time, I wouldn't have to try to find a time that suits you to spend time together." He even managed to look injured, like he was the wronged and thoughtful boyfriend trying to please a high-maintenance girlfriend who, despite his best efforts, he could never satisfy. Well, that was right in one respect. He had never satisfied her, not even close.

"Who are you kidding? If you wanted to spend time with me, you wouldn't have brought your friends. At least they had the decency to look embarrassed by your behaviour." She gestured towards the door, each venomous word lifting the oppressive weight from her shoulders.

"I don't have to stand here and take this. Call me to apologise when you're done PMSing, and clean this place up, it's a tip." Maya felt the prickling of tears as her hands balled into fists the moment he walked away, slamming the door behind him. The sound of her beating heart intensified the throbbing in her head.

Slipping the chain back into place, she noticed her digital flier on the telephone table had updated and was scrolling through the newest adverts, or more specifically, she noticed the advert for the locksmith currently being displayed. Before she had even had a chance to talk herself out of it, she was talking to the company, explaining that someone had a set of her keys and kept letting themselves into her house when she wasn't home.

A few hours later, she was on her way to

work with a fresh set of keys and a stomach full of rage. She deleted his messages, their pictures, purging him from her mind. They were done, and as guilty as she knew it should make her feel, she felt no remorse, only relief.

As her engine fell silent, she sat for a few seconds, attempting to calm herself, when her device chimed. She was waiting to hear back from Carley about the chances of a night out. Carley lived for the night scene. A succubus by nature, she thrived on the energy the clubs her mother owned generated, and they never had to queue.

The downside was they parted ways at the door but kept tabs on each other's safety. Since Maya almost never drank, and Carley knew how to protect herself, it was never really a problem. Maya went for the dancing, Carley for the sex and seduction. When she opened the message, Maya saw it wasn't her friend, but Rick. Against her better judgement, she opened it anyway.

Rick: *My key isn't working.*

Maya: *I've had the locks changed.* She fired off a quick reply as she locked her car. Her skin prickled again as she felt someone's eyes upon her. She kept her focus trained to her device, avoiding the temptation to look for the owner of the intense stare she felt.

Rick: Head past and drop my key off, I can't get in.

Maya: You're not getting a key.

Rick: If this is about this afternoon, you have to understand how much you humiliated me in front of the guys.

Rick: You there?

Rick: So since you're at work, again, maybe I can pick up my key instead?

Maya: You're not getting a key. We're done.

Rick: But I gave my notice on the flat.

Maya: And?

Rick: I wanted it to be a surprise, I'm moving in with you.

Maya: I suggest you recall your notice. I'm not looking for a roommate.

Rick: I thought we were more than that.

Maya: You've made it perfectly clear you're just looking for someone to clean up after you. I'm not your mother, and you're not moving in with me.

Rick: You have that right, you're way hotter than my mum. Look, I'll swing by your office for the key. I need some money for the taxi, so if you can leave it at the reception too, that'd be great. I've booked tomorrow off work so we can use your car to move my things in. Send me your work address.

Maya: Are you serious, you don't know where I work?

Rick: You're a switchboard operator or something, right?

Rick: May? You never talk about your work. How am I meant to know what you do?

With a frustrated growl, Maya powered her device off. *'You never talk about work,'* seriously? What he meant to say was he never listened to anything that wasn't directly centred around him. What had she even been thinking getting involved with him in the first place?

The truth was she knew the answer: she'd just felt so lonely, and after two-and-a-half years looking for Raiden, Rick had seemed like a nice distraction. He used to bring flowers, make lunch for her shifts, but while she still made the effort for him, he stopped bothering the moment he'd had his own key cut while she had been asleep. That should have been her first warning. But after so long alone, coming home to a place that felt lived in had been nice, even if she knew she was settling.

"Earth to Bambi, do you copy?" It took a few moments before she realised she was already standing in her uniform in front of her locker, with her fists screwed up as tightly as the balls of clothing she had thrown inside. She closed the door, turning to Mike with a weary smile that made him wince dramatically. "You okay? We're ready to roll out."

Tonight had been one of those nights. Part of her was grateful for the barrage of call outs, especially after unloading to Mike about how things had been not just going but crashing south with Rick. Everything she had been holding back, all her gripes, large and small, from the way he made her feel guilty about the smallest things, to finding other women's underwear in the bed.

It wasn't a one-sided confession though; she confessed to her own feelings towards him, how he had been nothing more than a substitute for the person she was missing. She saw Mike frown when she mentioned Raiden, no doubt having heard the rumours, but he said nothing, just like the rest of the crew when she had joined them.

He listened to her every word, letting her get it all out of her system before telling her she had been foolish to let Rick treat her like that. Even if she had felt like she was settling, she had still made the effort for him. His actions had earned him the moniker Rick the Dick, which brought a chuckle bubbling from her.

Since then, it had been one call after another. They were just pulling away from giving a lovely old gentleman stitches after he had managed to slice his fingers open grasping a knife from the sink the wrong way, when the warning alarm blared from their devices. These sirens were a call to arms, so to speak. A high-profile incident. At just one block from their current location, Mike didn't even wait for Maya to buckle in before they were careening down the streets towards the gentleman's bar.

Having replenished her bag on the ride, Maya leapt from the ambulance, parting the crowd as she pushed her way through the blacked-out doors, which someone secured open after she'd passed through. Her attention was on high alert, scanning the faces of the crowd. It was a large bar, packed to the brim with predominantly male patrons. Mingling amongst them, beautiful women dressed in skimpy and seductive attire handed out complimentary drinks, no doubt the owner's way of keeping things calm. Despite the extra sway to their hips, not a drop was spilt as they worked the crowd.

The strobing and coloured lighting usually focused around the stage had been turned off, leaving the room bathed only in the soft ambient lighting. Maya's vision scanned upward to the large balcony, which must have been evacuated since no one was looking down. She knew when things like this happened, people often flocked to see what the commotion was.

She knew this club, not that she'd been here herself, but it was one of the many Carley visited. Sometimes her best friend would dance on the very stage she was working her way towards. The music had stilled, causing the silence to ring through the air before an excited hush of morbid conversation followed her. She wove her way through the crowd towards a man who she assumed to be the manager, as he commanded his men and women to go and put his patrons at ease. He controlled the crowd well, keeping people away from the figure she could now see on the floor.

The patient's thick glasses were twisted across his narrow face, shaken from their perch by the violent seizures. A buxom blonde supported his head, her gemstone-adorned nails glimmered as she did the only thing she could to help Johnathon Jameson, the finance director of Overton, as he rode the waves of his seizure. Maya recognised him at once. He had been on the news just a few days back talking about how his new financial system rollout would hit crime where it hurt and help prevent money laundering. From the white foam bubbling from his mouth, it seemed someone hadn't liked what he had to say.

Relieving the terrified woman, Maya inserted the gastric suction tube into his stomach before her work device even confirmed there was poison in his bloodstream. At the same time, Mike applied a tab to his device, pricking the man's finger. The chorus of her and Mike's devices chimed in unison. Seconds later, he was beside her, injecting the counter-agent. She removed the tube, knowing even the small amounts of his stomach contents removed would help with recovery. Mike rolled the man to his side, keeping his airways open as he tested the blood again.

Their devices blared in warning, a sound so loud yet almost extinguished by the excited chatter of spectators as the figure before her grew limp entering cardiac arrest. Rolling him over, Mike pulled a CPR mask from his bag and began shielded breathing while Maya started compressions.

"Come on, beat," she whispered, feeling the heat from the stares prickle around her. The air was stifling, flooded with the scent of sweat and body lotions that made her want to retch. "Beat, beat, beat." Her device chimed, confirming a pulse. "That's it, let's get you back with the living." The next thing she knew, the gathering crowd screamed, scattering in all directions as they stampeded towards the exits.

It wasn't until the second shot was fired she realised what was happening.

The finance officer's body jerked as the bullet entered his leg, coating her in the erupting spray of arterial fluid. Without missing a beat, she flipped the table that was behind her to provide a makeshift shield as another shot rang out, blowing splinters into the air just inches before her face. "Mike, take cover," she ordered, dragging her bag closer to remove her clamps and scalpel as a fourth shot was fired. She glanced up, seeing that instead of doing as instructed, Mike had followed her lead, surrounding them with upended tables. The highly polished surfaces reflected the flashing lights of the Blue Coats' vehicles as they arrived outside.

"Not a chance. Tell me what you need."

Maya's training had been different to any other medics; she was the first person to ever move to the medics from surgery, and surgery had been something she'd taken a keen interest in for as long as she could remember. Her father had often joked to his colleagues that she had been born with a scalpel in her hand. Her father's honed skills saw him elevated to the hospital's head of surgery, and she knew from the moment she could read she wanted to follow in his footsteps.

She had been thought a child prodigy and studied and understood anatomy before she could even pronounce the words. She was the youngest surgeon to qualify on Mython. Her father had even pulled some strings and arranged for a twelve-month mentorship during her residency under the hospital's leading trauma surgeon.

After her father retired, they continued to practice techniques together on the life-like dummies. His doctors had said practising his hand-eye coordination could help to slow the disease's progress, but near the end he was content to watch his daughter at work, offering advice on techniques he had developed through decades of practice. Although his shaking hands were no longer able to perform tasks he had once executed without thought, his mind remained attentive, his advice sound.

"Fine, kneel here until I have the clamps in place, then keep an eye on his stats." Mike did as instructed as she made her incision, moving from one tool to the next as she parted skin and muscles, clamping either side of the now exposed artery. "Clear the blood, carefully." He grasped the gauze, dabbing the opening until the pooling of blood had been removed.

The muscular tube of the artery was barely held together. If not for her presence, there was no doubt this would have been a fatal injury. He would never have reached someone capable of saving him before he bled out. With steady hands, she removed the lodged bullet, placing it aside. Using a continual suture, she rejoined the artery together. Ensuring the suture's internal part went in the direction of the blood flow was as instinctive as her fluid movements.

There was nothing else in the world, not the screaming crowds or the bustle of the Blue Coats securing the area. It was just her and the patient. After tying off, she removed the clamps, checking the pulsatile wave both sides. Removing her gloves, she grabbed her medical scanner, checking for further injuries and confirming everything was as it should be while also visually examining for any seeping or leaking. Once the scanner confirmed everything was resolved, Mike helped her into fresh gloves, and she closed the wound.

Leaning back she turned her gaze to the ceiling, noticing someone possessed the foresight to turn one of the large unfiltered spotlights on them, and released a deep breath before returning her gaze to study her work. Her cheeks flushed as the sound of thunderous applause began to echo around her. Blue Coats kept patrons back outside of the table barrier in a wide circle, but she could see the devices held into the air, trained upon them. She felt her face grow hotter, realised Mike had stood, joining in the applause.

"Your father would be proud." It took the figure speaking for her to realise that, standing behind her, was her father's successor, Charlie Gilbert. When the notification of shots fired had sounded, he must have been called out to scene with it being a high-profile target. "Your turn." He gestured towards her, bringing her focus to the torn arm of her shirt where a spreading damp patch turned her green uniform black.

It was a glancing injury, but the gash looked as though someone had split her flesh with a knife and she hadn't even felt it. She felt the sting of the swab as he treated her, numbing the area. It took him only a matter of minutes to stitch the wound and apply the special gel that would accelerate healing. Anyone who had suffered minor injuries or donated via syphons at the Tap Houses would be familiar with this substance. There was a limit to what it could close, and this glancing injury fell outside of its margins. However, within three or four days she would just have a faint scar to show for her brush with death.

With her arm dressed, Maya flexed her fingers, rotating her arm and shoulder, still unable to feel anything. Thanking him, she moved to stand, surprised when she felt his firm hand pressing her back down onto the stool. "Take a moment. The Blue Coats want to take statements. I have to say, I'm impressed at how you remained so calm. Are you sure I can't poach you back? We miss having you in our theatres."

"Bambi's ours for keeps," Mike interjected, approaching with a gurney and one of the other team members in tow. He gave Maya an appreciative nod before turning his gaze towards the patient.

"Bambi?" Charlie laughed. It was a deep reverberating sound that once more took her back to her mentorship. "Well, with a name like that it's a good job you know how to treat gunshot wounds. Aren't you due your observed surgeries? I'll count this as one of them." Maya gave a weak smile as the head of trauma quizzed her. She knew all too well he knew exactly when she was due; he sent the reminder out personally every four months.

"Next month, but that would be great, thanks." Even though she had no immediate intention of returning to surgery, she kept her skills polished. She loved being a surgeon, and it was a way of staying close to her father, remembering the good times together where they would practice techniques and talk early into the morning. For them, standing with a surgeon's dummy between them was no different than a normal family watching a film. She missed him. Keeping this part of herself alive in some ways kept his memories fresh and, since today had been a day of honesty, she allowed herself to admit how much she truly missed being a surgeon, but it was a career she could not return to, not until she had answers.

"It's like you never stepped away. Do you still use his dummy?"

"You know I do." She grinned, glancing to her arm, certain when the adrenaline wore off it was going to hurt despite the gel. "Are you riding back with us?" she asked as another medic helped Mike transfer Johnathon Jameson onto the gurney.

"I'm riding with the Finance Director. I think you'll be some time behind me once you've finished giving statements. Good job there, Bambi. Your father would be proud." He had already begun to walk after the gurney as the praise fell from his lips, so she was glad he didn't see the tears his statement brought to her eyes this time.

"Hey, Bambi, doing okay?" Mike pressed a cup into her hand, bringing her attention towards the fact she was trembling ever so slightly. She stared at her hands as if they were betraying her; she never trembled. Then again, she'd never been shot at before either. Looking up from the glass, she gave him an incredulous look. "Hey, you're not going into shock, don't look at me like that."

"How about you, you doing okay, Stig?"

"I don't know how you kept so calm, but it kept me calm too. I'd say let's not mention it to Daisy, but with all the cameras pointing our way it seems impossible she won't find out." Mike nodded at the lingering Blue Coats waiting for their statements. At his cue, they approached, dragging some more stools and a table towards her.

Letting out a sigh, Blaze disappeared into the crowd, pulling his black hoodie over his hair. Storms and starlight, she had once called it, and even with an array of bottle colours and rainbow styles adorning many these days, his natural shades never failed to draw attention.

He rubbed a hand down his face. He couldn't believe this was happening; she wasn't meant to have been there. He had meant to be observing, making sure the hit-man did the job he had been paid for. Johnathon Jameson had been causing waves, and his new propositions, if rolled out, would make things run a little less smoothly for the Thorne family. His death was meant to be a warning. Lethal poison, showing that it didn't matter who or where you were, that you could still be silenced. But she just had to show up.

The balcony area had been closed for renovations, which made it the perfect place to ensure things went to plan, and if it didn't, then the assassin was on hand to deal the killing blow. Everything was going perfectly until Maya Jarrett arrived. The response time was too quick. They had calculated that with the two ambulances on call, no one would be able to arrive on scene in time for the counter-agent to be administered. Yet there she was, again, and before he had even flat-lined. Not that his dying stopped her.

The next thing he knew, their tracker chimed, confirming their target had a pulse. Three shots rang out. Blaze hadn't meant to intervene. Letting him line up the headshot despite the fatal arterial strike would have saved him a job, saved him following up on Jameson later since Maya had once again not let the dead lie. He was happy to watch him die, to let the assassin take care of business on his behalf, right until he realised Maya was the person in his sights.

He'd clearly realised this temptress would stop at nothing to save their target and had decided to remove the obstacle from the equation. Maya was an obstacle all right, but she was his. His to watch. His to torment. His to protect in his own roundabout fashion. He was the only one allowed to hurt her, him, no one else.

He knew the moment he pushed the barrel, there would be consequences, but he still hadn't been quick enough to still the trigger's movement. He had barely thrust the barrel aside when the trigger had been pulled. His gaze snapped to Maya, confirming she was uninjured. She was already digging around in the dead man's veins, repairing the damage. Her father would have been so proud to see how calm and focused she was despite the panic unfolding.

Following through, Blaze shoved the butt of the gun into the assassin's chin, dazing him enough to allow the curtain ties pulled from the blanketed windows to bind him. The Blue Coats would find him soon enough, and no one would know he was there, especially not the assassin.

Blaze shook his head, vanishing into the anonymity of the streets. Getting to Johnathon Jameson now he'd had an attempt on his life was going to be more difficult, but this time he would need to handle the details himself. He couldn't risk exposing what he already knew.

Sinking into the shadows in the corner of his favourite café, he called a greeting to Lewis before he pulled out his device, adding another name to the list. He thought she would have seen the pattern by now, but it seemed she was still overlooking the connection, just like the Blue Coats.

Now his targets were becoming high profile, it was going to get more dangerous, but he had made the world forget him once. If he was seen, he had no doubt no one would recall his presence. Being forgotten, however, didn't make accessing areas any easier. Memories could only be changed after the fact; he still had to move carefully.

Scanning down the list of names, he opened the tracking information for the next one on his list. Jerry Rushton. Maya had pulled him from a Road Traffic Accident six months ago. He had been unharmed, but his heart couldn't take the strain of the crash. It had been his time to move on. She hadn't let him pass peacefully; she had brought him back. Tonight that mistake would be corrected. Jerry Rushton would be laid to rest.

Closing his eyes, he relived the image of her in his mind, imagining the feeling of her lips on his skin. He drove himself mad with such thoughts. For months he had been toying with the idea of inserting himself into her life. It would make what he was doing now so much easier, but her boyfriend had made that impossible. Her boyfriend. That piece of scum who brought countless women to her home while she was working. If it wasn't the women, it was his friends, trashing the place and leaving her to clean up the mess. But as long as Rick was in her life, there could be no place for him.

He wanted all of her or nothing at all. There could be no half measures, not where she was involved. Her every kiss was branded on his heart, but she alone had been granted the release of forgetting everything they had been, of forgetting him.

CHAPTER 4

Maya gave a sigh, letting the steaming hot water of the station's shower wash over her. The heat over the waterproof dressing made her injury burn. While the locker room was unisex, the changing rooms were split, as would be expected, especially since the day staff had a more even male to female ratio. Hot jets of water massaged her tired muscles as she scrubbed the day's sweat and stresses from her body, if not her mind.

After the incident, she and Mike spent an hour with Detective Reuben Mendel copying the video data from the vehicle and personal cameras—which were tiny implants embedded in their belt buckles and collar pins—while being questioned about anything they witnessed as first responders to the incident.

Once they were released, Station Officer Silvers insisted they return to base for a critical incident stress debrief—or CISD—and some downtime. Still covered in blood, Maya took to the showers shortly after the debrief. She had to admit, after twenty-eight nights straight, coupled with today's events, she had never looked forward to having some days off quite so much before.

The Blue Coats said someone had apprehended the shooter on scene, rendering them unconscious and binding them. As she stood in the steam, her mind kept drifting back to the video footage. As she flipped the table, briefly, just before the fourth shot, the one that grazed her, she swore she saw a flash of silver hair concealed beneath a dark hood. A ghost. She knew better than to think it was anything else.

Each time in the past she thought she'd caught sight of him, she had allowed herself hope, only to be disappointed. Raiden was probably not the only person with hair the colour of storms and starlight, night sky and snow, but it was uncommon enough that she felt a slight electricity within her build each time she caught the slightest hint of silver in her vision.

With hair still wet, she changed into her jeans and tank top before flopping down on the common room sofa. Mike offered her a weary smile, the phone to his ear as he spoke to his wife in a soft and comforting tone, breaking the news of his encounter before she had time to turn on the television and witness the terrifying event herself.

Reaching for the remote, Maya turned the subtitles on. Recognising the article being about them, she rose to her feet. The news stations were all singing the praises of the medics who saved the Finance Director's life, speculating if not for their quick reactions, the director would have either died from poison or bled out. It went on to recount how he was dead for two minutes before being brought back, which was when the shots were fired. They even showed footage of the shooting. Maya felt herself pale, realising the first shot must have passed inches from her face. Watching herself on the screen like this seemed surreal. Her movements had been calm; she looked almost heroic, flipping the table and donning her gloves while Mike followed suit protecting them.

Once the images of Jameson being

transferred to hospital faded, they moved on to the next story. Overton's very own serial killer. He had been given the moniker Pyre-starter because his signature was burning his victims' corpses to ash. Having found no accelerants, they now believed they are looking for someone adept in fire magic. An image of a young woman appeared on screen as the reporter spoke of how this latest victim had been found just yesterday. Maya pushed herself to her feet, staring in horror at the picture, the same picture that had been delivered to her yesterday. She heard someone calling her, but the voice seemed so far away as her world descended into darkness.

Four faces seemed to float over her as she opened her eyes, and for one confused second, she wondered what they were doing in her home until she realised she wasn't home but lying on the floor of the common room. It was then her gaze flickered towards the television, recalling the news article. Her heart sped, and she felt as if she couldn't draw a satisfying breath.

"Hey, Bambi." Mike's voice sounded unusually soft. He crouched beside her. Her eyes opening seemed to be a cue for everyone else to step away. The news was just finishing up. She must have only been out for a matter of seconds. "You okay there?"

"That girl..." Maya pushed herself up, leaning with her back against the sofa. She winced as her aching arm protested the movement. Instead of prompting her when she trailed off, Mike waited, giving her time to get her thoughts into some semblance of order. "The girl on TV, someone sent me a picture of her yesterday. I didn't remember her until I saw it just, she was one of our patients."

"Which girl are you on about?" Mike questioned, glancing to the wall-mounted structure where the reporter was just signing off.

"Pyre-starter's latest victim. I was sent her picture yesterday." Maya ran a hand through her damp hair. It couldn't be a coincidence that yesterday she had received a picture of that girl and today she was dead. It just couldn't. With each second that ticked by, a horrifying reality set in. The envelope *had* been meant for her. What she didn't understand was why.

"Do you still have it?" Mike took her hand in his, trying to still the nervous energy that saw her run it through her hair time and time again.

"At home."

"Okay, now, are you hurt anywhere? You

went down like a sack of potatoes. Is your arm okay, your stitches?"

"I'm fine. Just shock, and the fact I've only had an energy bar all day." After the locksmith had come, it had been too late to fix herself something to eat, and their shift had been non-stop. No time to breathe, let alone swallow anything more substantial than the intermittent bites of a cardboard flavoured snack.

She sighed, finding it hard to believe it was only yesterday that she'd finally stood up to Rick. She glanced to the dressing on her arm. After another application of gel, the burning sensation should fade a little, and the lack of staining confirmed her little tousle with gravity hadn't caused any further damage.

"Right, that's it. I'm taking you home, we'll get some food in you and get the Blue Coats over. I don't like it, Maya." She knew he was serious; he'd used her name. "Why didn't you say something?"

"Honestly? When I saw it yesterday, I thought someone was trying to blackmail one of the neighbours, or Rick, about an affair. Why else would someone write 'STOP' on a picture?"

Mike passed his hand through his hair. "Give me your work device, I'll get yours, and we'll go."

She fished into the pocket, presenting it. The

medics had one rule. Personal devices were checked in at the door. Each shift was issued a work device coded for the shift in question, their own device being locked and docked in its place.

"It may be nothing, I'll ask them to send someone to meet us at your place."

Within thirty minutes, Mike pulled up outside her home, having grabbed a takeaway from the local cafe. Maya was grateful for the lift. She wasn't sure driving home would have been the safest option given how much her vision was swimming. But her vision hadn't needed to be sharp to make out the figure loitering by her door. She felt her hand freeze on the car for just a second. Head down, she marched towards him, leaving Mike to unload the food from the car. She was too exhausted to deal with Rick's nonsense right now.

"Oh, I see," he snarled, grasping her arm in the same way he had yesterday. She winced as he jerked her, causing her injury to burn. "You've not been working at all, have you? How long has this been going on?" Rick gestured wildly towards the car, his nostrils flaring as he saw Mike approaching with a bag of food in his hand.

"Not now, Rick." She tried to pull her arm free, but his grip tightened, causing her to suck in a breath between her teeth.

"Not now? I was meant to be moving in with you today. First you lock me out, then you bring someone else home."

"To lock you out, you'd have to be living here. You're not. Never will be. We're done. I'll leave your things on the porch; you can collect them later." She tried to keep her voice even, but she could hear the exhausted fury nestled within each syllable.

"You'd like that wouldn't you." He yanked on her arm, causing her to cry out as he pulled her closer so his snarling lips were at her ear. "Packing me off in boxes so you can fuck this guy. He's old enough to be your father, got some unresolved daddy issues there, May?" His grip sent splinters through her arm. "Here's what's gonna happen. You're gonna open the door, we'll go inside, and you can show me just how sorry you are for acting like a spoilt brat. When I think you've grovelled enough, I'll have the spare key, and we'll go get my things."

Just before the tears formed, before she could give him a piece of her mind, Mike slid up beside her, invading Rick's space in such a way he stepped away from Maya but didn't release her arm.

"Everything okay here, Bambi?"

"Rick was just leaving." She glared towards

him, yanking her arm from his grasp with a wince just as a detective's car pulled up. She saw him stiffen, his nostrils flaring as he recognised the markings on the vehicle.

"Are you kidding me, what kind of bitch calls the Coats on her boyfriend?"

"You're not my boyfriend, Rick, not anymore. Now I suggest you leave. Your things will be outside at five. I'll text Rob and let him know you need a ride, then I don't expect to see you again. Not ever."

He muttered something under his breath as he strode away she didn't catch, but with Detective Ruben closing in, he obviously thought better than to linger. It was only once he'd gone she realised her milk and orange juice must have been in the cloth bag Rick had snatched from the ground as he left.

Maya felt herself wilt slightly as Detective Reuben Mendel's stern hazel eyes glanced from the two photographs on her dining room table to her. It was only for a second, as he thanked her for the glass of lemonade she placed before him, but his gaze was unnerving.

This was only the second time she had seen

him smile since he arrived, something she found unsettling given the quantity of laugh lines clearly visible around his almond-shaped eyes. They told her he was a happy man, despite his reputation as one of the greatest homicide detectives in Mython. Yes, she had looked him up while she had excused herself to the kitchen to get them a drink. His stare was intense, stern in a way that would have even the innocent confessing their slightest misdemeanours.

She watched, hanging back just over his shoulder as his gloved hands once more raised the pictures, tracing his device over them. On the screen, several areas highlighted as they had the first time. This time, however, the small fingerprints began to vanish, removing Maya's from their results. Nothing. Not a highlight remained, not a smudge of a foreign substance, nothing. The envelope was the same story, with her fingerprints removed, one set remained, prints soon identified as Rick's, and a contaminate. The device began to run through similar matches until it settled on butter being the oily substance on Rick's fingers as he handled the letter.

"Can you think of any reason why you got these?" Pulling up a seat opposite him at the dining table, she pushed the stack of medical texts further across the table. The dining room was one room Rick never went in; he preferred to lounge in front of the television with a plate on his lap than sit for a meal. As such, she often used it as a study when she wanted to brush up on various things or read the latest papers, and leaving her things spread across the table guaranteed Rick wouldn't change his mind and begin using the room.

The thought of revealing this house did indeed have a study sat uneasily with her. She knew if he'd ever discovered the door to what he thought was the cleaning cupboard was, in fact, a staircase to the basement room, she would come home one day to find all her father's things destroyed and a new "man cave" in its place. She released a slow breath; he was gone now, she didn't have to censor her life.

"I thought one of the neighbours had been caught fooling around, or someone was warning my ex they knew what he was doing," she answered, shaking her head. Her pulse began to quicken as Detective Mendel reached to pull the latest envelope towards him, the one that had been waiting on the doormat when she had shown him inside. "It wasn't until I saw her picture on the news I realised it was something more. The other photo is she also—" Her words froze with a flinch as the envelope tore.

Detective Mendel tipped the contents onto his white evidence mat, something similar to a piece of fine towelling that collected any unseen particles so he could run it through analysis back at the station. Maya watched the photograph slide out, her hands cupping her mouth. "Gods, that's Jerry Rushton." The same red line crossed his face, the same scrawled warning, *STOP*. She didn't remember the face of everyone, but Jerry's family had stopped by the depot just two weeks ago to drop off a fruit basket in celebration of a birthday he wouldn't have had if not for their help.

"I think it would be better if we continued this conversation at the precinct," Ruben insisted as he placed the photos and the carefully folded evidence mat into a large zip-tie bag. As soon as he removed his gloves, he caressed his short stubble in thought, his gaze still on the opaque bag.

"You can't think she has anything to do with this?" Mike placed his fatherly hand upon her shoulder, squeezing softly. She was glad he had stayed. After the day she'd had, she wasn't sure she had the strength to see this through on her own. She glanced at the antique clock on the wall, the sway of its pendulum momentarily distracting her before she pulled her gaze to the clock face. A wave of guilt settled on her shoulders: Mike really should be home with his wife and baby, not babysitting her. She was a grown woman, after all.

"I'm afraid I'm going to have to insist. This doesn't sit well with me at all. You were shot at today, and now I find out you're getting these. Is it safe to assume the people in the photos were all your patients?"

Maya nodded, glancing to Mike for support. He had been the one to recognise the other woman.

"Look, she's not even been to bed yet, can she not come in the evening? It hasn't exactly been an easy day."

"No, I imagine not, but with this information, we need to explore the possibility that the Financial Director wasn't the target of today's shooting. We could be looking at an escalation. Clearly the killer feels some kind of connection to you. I'd feel better if you would come with me, and I need to show you some other photographs."

"Oh gods, there's more?" The news had only reported five victims.

"Fifteen. We have kept most of them quiet, and I would appreciate it if you'd do the same.

Before I arrived, I asked to have analytics run your whereabouts at the time of immolation. The good news is you have alibis for the murders." Detective Mendel scratched his chin again. She didn't need to be a genius to know there was something he wasn't saying, something he had seen in the photos she must have missed.

"I was a suspect?"

"The moment you came forward with these photos, we had to ensure you were who you said you were. Some killers like to insert themselves into the investigation. Fortunately for you, the events all occurred while you were on shift. Many while you were on an active call. We've had your S.O. send us your movement information so we can cross-check your whereabouts with your chip data." He must have seen her blanch because he offered the smallest of smiles. "It's routine. You wear cameras. Every call-out is tracked and logged. It's just due diligence. People like ourselves are openly trackable while on duty for our own safety. I'd be a fool not to use that data to firmly rule you out as a suspect."

"Can't you just access chip data to discover who's behind this?" Mike questioned, still gripping Maya's shoulder. When it appeared the detective wasn't going to answer, he spoke again, this time his question directed towards her. "Want me to come with you?"

"No, that's fine." Her voice didn't sound as strong as she would have liked. Her mind was still reeling at the thought the shots could have been intended for her. She found her fingers unconsciously stroking the dressing on her arm, sending a ripple of pain across her skin.

"One more question before you go." Mike raised his hand as Detective Mendel stood. "What did the shooter say?"

"Like most in his profession, he is suffering from selective amnesia."

Blaze dropped into the indicated seat at the deserted restaurant before being left alone. As cliche as it was for crime families to meet in such locations, all his important meetings occurred here. Occasionally they would seek him out for a job, but more often than not, he reported to them. When he had arrived home, a car had been waiting, bringing him straight to this quaint restaurant just outside the main city of Overton.

The venue's design had been well considered. Half had been segregated into a soft play area and indoor park, separated from a more sophisticated adult dining area by soundproof walls and heavy doors.

The family area had been Luiza's idea, her reasoning as calculating as the torture she so happily inflicted on others. Family dining was far less suspicious, and if required, the noise of excited children playing could drown out any whispered threats. It gave people a chance to dine out with their families and conduct business, but there was a darker side too. People were expected to bring their families here. It was a veiled threat, but an effective one.

Blaze fidgeted in one of the high-back chairs. These seats were not designed for comfort. Their straight backs forced an uncomfortable amount of posture correction while the metal studs decoratively adorning the lush velvet fabric had no qualms about digging into his flesh. These weren't chairs, they were subtle contraptions of torture.

"It is about time you showed. Do you want to explain why I have an assassin in cuffs and a hit still walking?"

Blaze straightened. He should have known the boss would come in person. Most of their dealings over the last three years had been face-to-face. Despite his senior years, Mr Thorne stood ramrod straight, the greying to his black hair serving only to add a distinguished look to his softly aged features.

No one knew exactly how old the Thorne patriarch was, but he had recited many stories from before the barrier's erection, before the divide of the world. It was a common misconception that vampires didn't age; they did, but at an incredibly slow pace. It was an easy mistake to understand. Their longevity was like comparing the lifespan of a firefly to that of a Greenland shark. To the firefly and its children, the shark would seem ageless. It was all about perception.

"It was a real shit show, boss. I thought he was meant to be a pro."

"He was one of my best."

"Could have fooled me." Okay, he knew he could be brazen, that the boss appreciated his coarse manner, but maybe that had been a little too much. "The guy was wired before he even entered the place. Everything was against him. The medics were on scene quicker than anticipated, forcing him to take matters into his own hands. But out of four bullets, only one of them even struck the target."

"I saw the footage." Blaze swallowed at the boss' terse reply. "What I don't understand is why there weren't more shots taken since he'd already blown his cover. Why didn't he take out the medic and realign the shot?"

"After the fourth shot, the Blue Coats probably had sights on him." Not a lie as such but a media truth, one the television had provided him with when the news reported the Blue Coats had rushed on scene apprehending the shooter before they could fire any more shots.

"And where were you?"

"Ground level. When I got the ping to say his heart restarted, I was going to..." Blaze wiggled his fingers meaningfully. "You know a quick jolt to keep it subtle. But it was too risky, the place was swarming. I removed myself from the scene before I could be detained for questioning."

"Our lawyers got to him before he could be made to say anything too incriminating."

"Did he explain what happened?" He saw his boss' lips twitch, a microscopic movement, but one that confirmed his response had been correct. So, he had been suspected. The boss wondered if he had intervened. His question was bait to see if Blaze wondered if the assassin would reveal something damning about his own involvement. What the boss didn't realise is he had no need to worry about his actions being revealed; they weren't remembered. His lack of concern, the lack of any small bodily responses, told the boss he was innocent of any deception. Mr Thorne was a human lie-detector. No one could lie to him. No one but Blaze.

"Nothing. The lawyer says he's claiming amnesia. He'll keep his mouth shut, but we still have a situation that needs remedying."

"I'll deal with Jameson personally."

"Speaking of your personal touch, are you any closer to finding the identity of the person we're looking for?" The boss ran a finger across the polished surface of the table before glancing to it.

"I've neutralised five targets, but as yet none of the data is collaborating." All truth. The key to lying was to tell the facts in a way that the listener drew their own conclusions.

"Very well. Keep looking. You know how important it is for you to find them and bring them to me. The car is waiting to take you home." With those words, Mr Thorne turned on his heel and departed, and Blaze wasted no time in returning to the car.

Blaze sat back into the soft upholstery of the car seat. The raised privacy partition allowed him some measure of isolation. Closing his eyes, he pretended to sleep, but his mind was too active.

Everything that happened now was because

of a mistake he'd made a few weeks ago. He had kept his quiet rectifications of Maya's actions secret, quiet from anyone who may have noticed or taken an interest in her perversion of death. Normally, anyone from the family seeing him work turned a blind eye, but not Luiza. She loved torture. Thrived on it. When she happened upon him in the dark alley, his actions appealed to her sadistic side. She had stayed to watch.

That was when he started with the pyres as an announcement of his deeds. He put on a show for Luiza, burning the person alive before she had time to realise what had been wrong. Or so he'd thought, but he could tell by the glint in her eyes that came from more than the burning embers, that she'd recognised his target for what they were. She was too intuitive. It had left him no choice but to go to the boss and reveal what he had uncovered.

He had kept his revelation short. Explaining how he became aware of this person and confirmed his suspicions while trying to rectify the mistake. He claimed this person was the first he had placed upon a pyre, still the truth, the others had been handled more carefully. There had been ten others before this. Ten dealt with in a more discrete manner. This revelation, however, still had the feared results. His boss now wanted the person responsible for the lives Blaze had put to flame. He'd given Blaze free rein but was expecting results.

With five deaths now attributed to Pyre-starter, he didn't know how much longer he could claim dead-ends in his investigations. Especially when Maya had been caught on camera resuscitating the latest hit. It was only a matter of time before eyes turned to her. He would have to watch her more closely, encourage her to heed his warning. She needed to stop, and soon.

He had not sacrificed everything he had for her to become their target again.

CHAPTER 5

Hours passed, and by the time she was allowed to leave, Maya felt more like a suspect than someone being questioned in the hope of gaining a lead. She was exhausted, and if she had to sit through another round of *how many times can we phrase the same question a different way*, she was going to scream or cry. Because as much as she hated to admit it, she was an angry crier, and she had reached the end of her tether.

She couldn't tell them what she didn't know. She had no enemies, or hadn't thought she had, and as far as she was concerned the only person with a reason to be frustrated with her at the moment was her no-good ex, Rick.

Whilst she had finally admitted that he was a grade-A arsehole, she knew he wouldn't resort to murder for two reasons. Firstly, it was too much effort, and secondly, he had made it perfectly clear he had no idea what she actually did for a living, so the chances of him tracking down people she had saved were next to none.

Detective Mendel had been polite enough, asking his questions softly while ensuring she had water, coffee, even snacks, but his intensity was exhausting. Part of her couldn't help but wonder if he hoped she would become so tired she slipped up and confessed to the murders herself. A part of her, the part desperately craving sleep, even thought this might be a good idea, especially since she already had alibis.

"We are about done now, Miss Jarrett. I must apologise for keeping you so long, but there is one final thing I need you to do for us." Detective Mendel's voice startled her. He had left a few moments ago, and she'd made the mistake of resting her head on the white interrogation room's table.

"What?" she asked on an exhale. She saw a look akin to sympathy cross his features.

"You can refuse, but I've had the shooter moved to the adjoining interview room. I want you to look through the one-way mirror and see if you recognise him."

She gave a weary nod, pushing herself to her feet, forgetting to cringe as the chair scraped across the tiled floor with a loud screech.

Maya did as asked. She looked through the glass long and hard, studying his angular face, his dark eyes and buzz-cut blond hair. She even noticed the small mole on his left cheek and the start of stubble, naturally a few shades darker than his hair. What she didn't see, however, was someone she recognised, which left her with a confused sensation, unsure whether she should feel relieved or not.

"I don't know him," she stated after staring at him for several long minutes, imagining his hands on the gun, his sharp eyes watching her down the weapon's sights. Her hand tentatively touched the dressing on her arm. Had he been aiming for her? Her mind flipped between the cross-hairs being pointed at her and the Financial Director. He seemed the more likely target; she was nobody. Then again, someone had sent her those photos. Could she be looking at Pyre-starter?

"Thank you, Miss Jarrett. As I mentioned before, I don't believe you were his target, but it wasn't a possibility we could ignore."

"What about Pyre-starter?"

"I've a team working on cross-checking your patients against the recent murders. It's too early to know anything for sure. It could just be someone who has made a connection between you and three victims and thinks you're responsible. Why else warn you to stop?" She had to admit he made a good point. The words seemed out of place to her even now. "We will look into it, and have a patrol watching your door this next week to see if they can catch sight of whoever is delivering the envelopes. Do you have someone you can call to take you home? If not, I could—"

"My friend Carley's on the way, but thanks." She had messaged Carley the moment she left the interrogation room, and her friend had confirmed she'd be straight over. They hadn't seen as much of each other as Maya would have liked this month because of Maya's long stretch, but she knew Carley would come at the drop of a hat whenever she was needed, and right now, she needed a friend, not a stranger in a taxi.

"It may be prudent not to stay alone, just for a few nights."

"Thank you, detective." Even as she spoke, she saw the shimmer of Carley's ombre brown-to-golden shoulder-length curls. Her friend always looked like she glided straight from a party girl catwalk. Her denim shorts were just long enough not to be indecent, while her one-size-too-small crop top stretched across her ample bosom, showcasing her almost flat stomach. She was sex on legs, and what legs she had, perfectly accentuated by her killer six-inch stiletto heels.

"Bambi," she intoned, her bracelets jangling as she raised her arms for a hug. Carley had, unfortunately, heard about her nickname and decided to hop on the bandwagon despite them knowing each other for years. In fact, it was thanks to Carley she had met Raiden.

They had been out for a night on the town to celebrate Maya's new residency. As always, men were falling over themselves to get to the stunning succubus, as they often did. They had been separated on the dance floor when a set of hands rested upon her hips, gliding her away from the pervert who had been grinding a little too close.

She had never forgotten the way his hands felt on her hips, like they were made to be placed there. He met her moves step for step, teasing just enough to raise her pulse, his movements so fluid their dance could have been choreographed. On the dance floor, it was as if her body had always known him. '*Leave with me now,*' he had whispered into her hair. Her heart raced before she had even turned, ending their seductive play, and against all her better judgement, she had done just that. The music playing had become their song, and to this day it was still played at the party venues, although now she danced alone, her eyes always closed imagining he was with her.

"Thanks for coming, you have my contact information, and remember what we talked about." He tapped his belt buckle, reminding her she was to start wearing her uniform belt whenever she was out, just in case they saw something useful on the cameras at a later time. Despite the depot dry cleaning the uniforms in house, she always kept one at home, just like everyone else, for those times when large accidents rocked the community and all hands were called on deck to meet at the scene.

"How you feeling?" Carley questioned, linking her arm through Maya's as she guided her outside. The fresh air was a welcome reprieve from the stuffy precinct, the autumn wind blowing away just a measure of her fatigue.

"Tired." She rubbed her hands over her bare arms as she felt her skin prickle, causing her to cast a tired gaze across the almost empty car park.

"Right, I'm gonna get you home, put you to bed, and hijack your TV. I'm taking you out tonight. You look in need of some serious stress relief."

"Thanks." As Maya sank into the high-quality upholstery of Carley's newest car, the tension seemed to drain from her. "Oh, I have a new key for you." Maya fished into her purse, placing a small envelope with her name on the dashboard.

"Finally. I thought Rick was going to be freeloading on you forever. I don't know why you put up with him for so long."

"Just lonely I guess," she whispered, her thoughts once more returning to Raiden. The anniversary of his disappearance haunted her more than usual.

Blaze watched from the shadows as Maya emerged from the Blue Coat headquarters with Carley. He couldn't help the way his gaze was drawn to her. Even as exhausted as she looked, she was still stunning. It made him ache for the days he had woken up beside her in the evening light. When they had first met in one of the dance clubs, it had been as if a spotlight shone down upon her, causing all else to fade into the background.

Yes, the meeting had been prearranged by someone else, but nothing about her had been planned. She had taken his world by storm. The moment he touched her, he became undone in the most bitter-sweet way imaginable. There was nothing he wouldn't have done for her, nothing including sacrifice his heart, and that was exactly what he had done three years ago. He had destroyed himself to save her.

After he stole her away from the club, they had gone to a dessert parlour, a place where they could actually hear each other talk beyond the language of their bodies. He hadn't been given much information, only that her father was a surgeon for his boss.

He remembered how he smiled to himself as she spun a line about starting her surgical residency. She was not the first woman to embellish to gain his attention. He thought she would realise her age betrayed the fib, but he'd been intrigued by her beyond his assignment. She was captivating in mind and body. Whenever her hand lightly touched his arm as she spoke, he felt a tingle of electricity, as if the lightning within his veins rose to meet her touch.

He still remembered how his heart lurched when a call came through. Her carefree smile morphed into a look of abject horror as the colour drained from her face. She had dashed from the building with a quick apology and straight into an idling taxi outside. His first instinct was to wonder if that had been her safety phone call, a reason to excuse herself, but something about her expression, the way she had moved, told him otherwise.

About five minutes later, the news on the television behind the counter interrupted the music channel, talking about a building collapse with hundreds thought to be trapped inside while those already pulled from the rubble were on their way to hospital. He knew then what the call had been, and perhaps understood why she was one of the few people at the club who only drank water.

Having not exchanged contact details, their second date had been a little harder to plan. He turned up at the hospital twelve hours after she left him, armed with a coffeemaker and picnic basket of food. It was perhaps a foolish gesture, but bringing her hot coffee when she was likely stuck in surgery seemed pointless. This, he thought, at least bordered on a romantic gesture.

They had only exchanged first names, but he knew her from the information he had passed. Still, he played the fool, telling the receptionist it was a gift for Maya, showing a picture of them together he'd had the foresight to take. Fortunately, the woman had known who he meant and promised she would deliver the gift personally.

Inside the basket had been a selection of foods, including energy bars, chocolates, fruits, sandwiches, a selection of coffee, and most importantly, his number. When his phone rang three days later, he thought he'd been given the world.

Maya had done so much good in her life, saved so many, but now he was dedicating his life to undoing everything she had accomplished. She should have stayed in surgery. It was the role she had been born for. Why she had transferred to the medics, he would never know. As much as he wanted to pry, he knew better than to start asking questions. Questions earned attention, and cameras recorded everything inside the hospital.

Once Carley's car was no longer visible he checked his device. He had crossed two more names from the list. One he had needed to take care of; the other was spared his intervention. He was always careful to ensure she could not be incriminated by his actions. He wanted to protect her, but the truth was, once he reached the end of his list, he would have no choice but to take care of the one responsible. Her.

The only reason she still walked around was because he had lied, claimed he didn't know who was behind these deeds. It was only a matter of time before they realised it was her. After all, if he had discovered the pattern, anyone could. But he just couldn't bring himself to do what must be done.

If she would just stop what she was doing the trail would go cold. She would be safe.

Maya smiled at her reflection in the inbuilt mirror on her wardrobe door. She slipped on her silk red halter-neck top and appreciated the way it clung to her feminine curves. The way it whispered against her skin made her feel something she hadn't felt for a long time, sexy. When paired with her pleated skorts, she knew even standing next to the glamorous Carley, she would still look good. The short length was enough to be teasing, while the sewn-in shorts allowed her freedom to move without having to worry about the skirt flaring up as she spun. It had been too long since she had last danced, last lost herself to music.

She finished applying her smoky makeup, loving how the colours made her eyes seem even darker and larger than normal. Carley styled her hair so she could leave it down, tsking as she saw the bobble left around her wrist. Maya knew from experience loose hair and dancing wasn't a recipe for success, but in the interest of looking her best, for the first part of the night at least, she had surrendered to Carley's instruction, also removing the dressing to avoid a glowing patch on her skin under the club lights. The reddening of the area had already drastically reduced thanks to the gel, and the sutures were barely visible against her creamy skin.

"Wow, you look stunning," Carley commented, letting herself into Maya's bedroom. Maya looked to her friend in awe. Every woman wanted to own a little black dress that looked like the one her friend wore. Carley always had the latest fashions, and there wasn't a second of the day, even first thing in the morning after an energetic night, where she didn't look like a goddess. "'Those single lads won't know what hit them." She fanned herself, bringing a smile to Maya's lips.

"Thanks, but I'm not looking for anything more than a dance to burn off stress."

"I can think of plenty of ways to burn off that nervous energy you're carrying." Carley waggled her perfectly shaped eyebrows, causing the slight application of glitter to sparkle.

"Behave. I don't hook up with random strangers."

"Oh, you wound me." Carley placed her hand above her heart. "A girl's got to eat. Speaking of which, are you sure you want to grab a cab? We can take your car, that way I won't have to worry about you getting home." The offer coming from anyone else would sound like she had been nominated to be designated driver, but Carley knew Maya rarely drank. It was something that dated back to her time as a surgeon. Dancing was her way of unwinding, but she didn't need alcohol as a buffer. She had no qualms about looking like a fool on the dance floor as she lost herself to the music. It was the best stress relief she knew, save for one.

"I'll probably leave shortly after you get your midnight delight anyway," she answered, shaking her head. Carley always left once she'd secured her prey, and Maya usually left just after. After the day she'd had, she wanted the option to have a drink if the mood took her, and she was not one to drive if even a drop of alcohol had touched her lips.

The taxi driver was still checking them out in the rear-view mirror as he drove away, meaning Carley stood there for longer than necessary, posturing slightly, gaining the attention of not only the driver but the long line of people waiting to be granted admittance into the club. The enormous line spanned around the side of the building.

Teasers was the most popular party destination, with people sometimes waiting hours just to get in. But they didn't need to worry about that. Carley marched them straight up to the VIP rope, easy, instant entry. It helped that her mother owned the clubs, but there hadn't been a VIP event she hadn't managed to gain entry to yet.

The place thrummed with energy and music, the entrance split into three different dance rooms, each with their own bar and musical theme. The sound-proofing between the areas was state of the art, ensuring no bleed, just like in the quiet rooms above, where patrons could go to enjoy a quiet drink or relax when things got too loud. Tonight's themes were pop, heavy metal, and dance. With a wink, she and Carley went their separate ways. She loved her friend, but watching her lure unsuspecting prey was something she didn't need to see.

"Message me if you need me." Carley waved her device meaningfully. When they went out like this, they activated Tracking-Mate, an app designed to allow you to find your party partner, or send a quick SOS with a predetermined tapping of the screen. Not that they ever needed such things.

Events like this were heavy on the muscle, and breach of conduct rules, such as persistent unwanted advances, saw people removed from the property with a temporary ban. Generally, people behaved. It only took moving away from someone on the dance floor for them to set their attentions on someone else. It was one of the things she liked about coming to these places. It was busy, charged, but most importantly, it felt safe to dance and let loose without having to worry about creeps getting too handsy.

Usually, she would frequent the dancing scene, but tonight she found her hands upon the pop music door. Pushing it open she was assailed by smoke, mirrors, and coloured lights as the rhythmic beats washed over her, sweeping her up before she had even made her way to the dance floor.

Her steps already bounced as she wove into the crowd, finding a space to claim as her own. Eyes closed she began swaying, hearing the music, feeling the beat as her feet slowly began to move. Her shoulders swayed as she used her hips and arms to extenuate every movement she made, the niggling pain of her arm all but forgotten.

She didn't care that she probably looked ridiculous, she felt free. What she didn't realise was she by no means looked like she didn't belong. If she'd had her eyes open, she would have realised how much attention her dancing attracted.

Maya thought Carley looked like sex on legs. What she didn't realise was the reason Carley always parted paths when on the hunt was that even a succubus couldn't hold a candle to her when it came to dancing. The way she moved and lost herself to the music so completely was nothing short of erotic. Her heels slid, her hands traced parts of herself the onlookers longed to touch. She looked like a goddess. But she didn't notice that; she just allowed herself to feel, to dance, and for all the stress of the last few days to be washed away by her movements.

CHAPTER 6

*B*laze slipped the D.J. a few notes from his pocket. The man nodded, confirming their standing agreement. Whenever Maya went dancing, he was there. He would pay the D.J. to play a song, their song, the one that made him think of her, and from the way she moved, he could almost believe that she was thinking of him too.

He allowed himself this one indulgence as he watched her from afar, separated by the crowd, and yet it was like she was the only person there, lights flashing as her curves teased him. It was like the first time he had seen her all over again, but with one difference, he knew it could never be. He had deliberately made her forget everything they were, everything they had and could be, their plans, their love, everything, and not a day went by where he wished there had been another way.

His skin bristled as he saw her recently ex-boyfriend dancing towards her, a sleazy grin on his face as he bopped his head in time to the music. There was something almost practised about the way his steps wove between the dancers, two glasses lifted in the air, not spilling a drop.

The way she tensed as he began to dance around her, leaning too close, whispering into her hair in the way he had once done. Even from where Blaze stood, lost within the crowd, he could see the look of incredulity as she opened her eyes, seeing who was responsible for the unwanted touching.

His lips moved, mouthing something that looked a lot like the word truce as he offered the drink. She eyed it cautiously, but accepted, tipping her glass to his before downing the shot and returning the glass. Turning her back and walking away, she thread herself through the crowd, but the snake slithered behind her, depositing the empty glasses somewhere on his journey.

He caught up with her, his arms snaking

around her before she pushed him away and spun carefully away into another space on the dance floor. But he followed, grinding against her in an obviously unwelcome fashion. It was at that moment the D.J. played their song, and the thought of Rick touching her through something which was theirs infuriated him.

His feet carried him across the dance floor before he had time to think. People cleared a path, and the lights lit his way, until his goddess stood before him, her back towards him as she danced, lost to their song, her hands moving as if remembering his touch. As Rick reached out again, Blaze's hands cupped her hips, using a gentle pressure to guide her away. The glare he shot towards Rick saw him bow out, disappearing back into the crowd for the moment at least, but that left him with another problem. Maya was in his arms.

He had fantasised about doing just this each time he'd seen her dance, but memories and imaginings paled to the reality of even this most innocent touch. He groaned quietly as she leaned into him without even glancing over her shoulder. He swore he heard her whimper as his arms encircled her, keeping her back to him despite her efforts to turn. She pivoted, only to be spun around before she could catch sight of his face. She traced her body against his, reminding him how perfectly they had once fit together.

Reaching behind her, she squeezed his buttock, pulling him closer, teasing him as much as he was her. She raised her arms, her hand tracing down his jaw as she lowered herself down, causing his hands to trace up her hips and side, the soft fabric of her top teasing his fingers as he breathed in the scent of her hair. Her fingers met his, interlocking them together as she guided his hands over her seductively, making him ask why was he doing this to himself, why he didn't just step away and spare himself this torture.

She pivoted again, turning gracefully on her heel. He could see the frustration in the way her shoulders stiffened as his careful glide positioned him just beyond her sight before he grasped her again, pulling her back into him. The heat of their bodies sent sparks of electricity flying back and forth, energising him in a way that had only ever happened when they were together.

Hypnotised by the sway of her body, the momentum of her movements, he found himself envisioning their future. Her steps became more passionate, more desperate as she kept trying to catch a glimpse of him. But he knew her body well enough to predict her every glance, her every sway. He buried his head into her hair, his hot breath causing goose pimples to chase down her neck. How he'd missed touching her, being this close. The song was coming to its end, and his chest tightened, knowing this could never be any more than just one dance. But he wanted more. Now she had been in his arms again, he feared he didn't know how to let go.

"Leave with me now." He regretted the words as soon as they slipped from his lips in a voice filled with desire and need. She was everything he had ever wanted, and that was exactly why he had to leave. He felt her freeze in his arms, but by the time she turned, he had already used the crowd to vanish, putting a distance between them that now seemed charged with his own heartache.

He wondered for a moment if she could feel his sense of loss, if she could follow the feelings straight to his heart, straight to him. He watched her standing there, her eyes bright with what looked to be tears as she desperately searched the dance floor, pushing her way through the crowd. He saw the dampness on her cheeks that came from more than just sweat, and his heart ached.

Her shoulders slumped in the way they did when she was hurt, her confident gaze lowering to the floor as she left the dance floor. But there was more in her gait than dejection, and the haunted look in her eyes seemed to be something more than the loss of a dancing partner. He had to be mistaken, projecting his own feelings of loss onto her. She didn't know him. Unlike him, she had no idea of what they had lost.

She sat at the bar, the barkeep instantly veering towards her to fill her order. Once, twice, three times she knocked back shots in a way he had never seen her do before. Again and again, she ordered until her ex once more encroached. Another drink was pressed into her hand, words exchanged Blaze couldn't hear as she glared at him before knocking it back. He watched in dismay. He knew Maya, his hands remembered her every contour, his soul recognised hers. What he didn't recognise at this moment was what she was doing. Maya didn't drink, not like this.

The electricity of his touch lingered on her skin, charging her clothes with a static that was almost like his fingertips caressing her. She had felt herself gasp as the firm hands grasped her hips confidently, as if their owner knew they fit together, as if he'd held her that way a thousand times before. She'd closed her eyes, letting him guide her away from Rick, who, despite his call of truce, seemed to think that meant he was once more a part of her life.

She had closed her eyes for a moment, imagining the stranger to be Raiden, pairing his movements to the first dance they had shared. It had been their song that was playing, his actions, their dance. The one they always had enjoyed whenever they went out together. But compared to her memory, this touch seemed real, familiar, like a dream made flesh. The urge to see his face became all-consuming. No longer lost to the memory, she became convinced if she were to turn she would find herself in his arms, looking up into his ice-blue eyes. She needed to look, to prove to herself it wasn't him, to prove to herself it was.

The way his hands traced her, how sparks sang with each touch, only Raiden had made her feel like this. He played her body like a finely tuned instrument, predicting and intercepting her every movement with his provocative seduction. Unable to see him she tried to map his face with her hands, imagining her fingers dancing between strands of storms and starlight before feeling the soft burn of stubble as her open hand traced his skin, but the contours of his oblong face did nothing to dispel the illusion. It sang of a face known by something other than sight, and it felt painfully familiar to her touch.

So she lost herself to the fantasy, locking his fingers with hers, imagining it was Raiden who touched her with fervour and passion, whose hot breath tickled her ears, leaving the lingering scent of winter frost as he whispered huskily with desire the words she'd longed to hear, *'Leave with me now.'* It had taken a moment for her to realise she'd actually heard the words, heard his voice.

By the time she turned, he was gone, but he left something in his place, fresh heartbreak. She searched the crowd, but he had vanished, again. A ghost, a dream. Sweet torture. No, there was nothing sweet, just torturous. She pushed her way through the crowd, hoping to catch sight of her phantom, but such creatures were nothing if not evasive. He had vanished in a puff of steam from the smoke machines and the grinding of bodies. Life went on with its pumping and grinding, and no one noticed her world had stopped.

Never before had she needed a drink. But as

her breathing refused to calm she found herself at the bar, her chest aching as she chased away the tears with strong, neat chasers that were weaker by far than the burn of her grief. Knocking back drink after drink, she tried to punctuate each one with a breath, reminding herself to breathe. With each drink came a breath, and soon the ache in her chest began to dull, and her breathing calmed.

"Share one with me." Rick smiled, pressing another drink into her grasp. She wasn't sure how long he had been standing there, but the smirk playing on his lips suggested he'd witnessed her crashing descent. He placed his hand on her face. "Don't cry over me, May. I forgive you."

Cry? Was she crying? She tried to raise a hand to her cheeks, but he grabbed her wrists, pulling her towards him, forcing his lips to hers, his hands roving over her body, sullying all the places her ghost had touched.

Blaze watched furiously as her sleazy ex—who had already struck out with at least three women tonight—pulled Maya towards him, forcing his lips to hers. He watched her just stand there, tears streaking her cheeks as he kissed her, his hands wandering over her body in a way that made Blaze want to break each and every one of those offending fingers.

For a moment, she stood frozen until her mind seemed to register what was happening. She thrust her hands against his chest, pushing him backwards before stumbling away. He didn't need to have seen how much she had drank to know she'd had too much. She staggered from table to pillar, plotting a twisted route to her escape.

"Find Carley," he whispered as he saw her reach the door. He knew that look in her eyes; she was done. She needed space, air, but air right now would only further hinder her judgement. She needed to find her friend, she needed someone to look after her, make sure she got into a taxi safely. "Don't leave."

There was something in the way Rick smiled as she left that set him on edge. By the time he reached the exit, Maya was nowhere to be seen, and Rick had already moved on to his next target. Blaze wanted to purge the world of his bane right now. Maya was not a throw-away conquest. She was not someone to be forgotten when another short skirt sauntered past. She was for keeps, forever, even if only to be worshipped from afar. That Rick didn't see this was a crime worthy of death.

The bouncer who lifted the rope for him confirmed having seen Maya, but not before he'd convinced him he wasn't some deranged stalker seeking to take advantage of an intoxicated young woman. The large man had actually smiled as Blaze logged into his account, showing a picture of the two of them camping within the mountains. He had taken all these memories from her, but he had not been able to let them go. He had stored them in the safest way he knew, an account no one could find, let alone link to him. The same place he saved all the incriminating information he came across, information that would prove useful in the future.

The streets were quiet, as would be expected at two in the morning. Even the streetlights had dimmed to a more ambient shade. The occasional bout of laughter from pubs and clubs carried on the wind from distant venues. The night was cool, autumn had arrived, and with it, the brilliant stars above shone down, creating a canvas of majesty that made every creature feel small. The rustle of shed leaves was punctuated with the wind's whispers as it tried to tease free more of the changing leaves.

He saw a figure in the distance, her hand outstretched to trace the walls which seemed to fight to keep her upright. Why hadn't she called a taxi outside, why was she always so darn stubborn? He knew she was going to the taxi rank. He would keep an eye on her until she was inside, trying not to think how the entry she would walk through passed his own front door. He bit his lip, imagining catching up with her, wrapping his arms around her waist and dragging her into his home, back into his arms where she belonged. He could claim her again, make her love him again, but as much as he wanted these things he would be her destruction, and being in her life would be her end, one way or another.

For the last three years, he had never brought a woman home, never engaged the same woman more than twice. He could have no weaknesses, that was why she'd had to go. But now his past and present collided. Maya was in danger no matter his decision, and he was the one she should fear, but soon it wouldn't be just him. Could he make himself believe that he could better protect her by her side? Of course he could. The problem was he had dedicated the last six months of his life to destroying her work, to killing those she had saved.

Dammit.

Before he could even convince himself he could make it work, that he could be beside her and still complete his mission, he saw a dark figure follow her into the entry.

"Purse and jewellery." The deep voice echoed through the darkness of the entryway from behind her. The scant lighting was not enough to see much, but what he could see was that Maya was on her knees. Her arms outstretched as she dropped her purse. He watched her slow movements as she removed her earrings and ring. "And that," the voice demanded. It was then Raiden realised she had something still clutched within her hand.

"No, please, it's not worth anything." The way she begged made his skin burn. He was the only one who should make her beg. Her fist clenched tighter.

"Then you shouldn't mind handing it over."

"No, I—" The sound of him striking her echoed down the small entryway. As she hit the floor, a small silver bracelet flew from her grasp, catching the lightning from Blaze's fingers.

No one hurt Maya.

The man screamed as the lightning streaked

in a manner that had taken much training to control. Somehow, despite his anger, it remained enough to render his victim unconscious without burning them from the inside out like his pyre victims. When dealing with them, he unleashed the full fury of the storm. Such was the only way to truly destroy a body in the way it had needed to be done. That was one thing the authorities had got wrong. Despite how he posed the remains, he didn't burn them on a pyre, he scorched them from existence.

Gathering her belongings, he slipped the jewellery into her bag, wondering why she would part with everything without a fight, everything except the bracelet. He recognised the silver chain as being one of the items that had once belonged to her mother, but so too were the rings and earrings she had removed without a thought. Of all the things, it held the least value. He scooped it into her purse along with the other items, not really paying attention to any of them. All that mattered now was getting her off the street.

Lifting her into his arms, he carried her further down the ally, glancing over his shoulder before opening the door to his flat using his swipe card. Most places recognised the tenants by their chip, but Blaze didn't have a chip. No one working his kind of job did. It was more damning than convenient, especially since, as far as anyone but the Thorne family was concerned, Raiden Blaze did not exist.

Placing her bag beside her on his bed, he watched her sleep for a moment. His fingers twitched, fighting back the desire to reach out and wipe away the trace of blood from her lips, to stroke her hair, to kiss the stitches in her arm from an injury he hadn't even realised she'd received until watching the reruns on the news.

It pained him how close that final bullet had been, that it still grazed her skin despite his intervention. He wanted to kiss away her pain, but if he did that she might wake, and one thing he couldn't afford was for her to find him here.

Reaching a bottle of water from one of the shelves inside his wardrobe, he placed it on the bedside table, scrawling a note with a penmanship she wouldn't recognise before leaving. She could let herself out. It was better for him if their paths didn't cross.

Their dance had been fun. It had taken him back to a time of possibilities, but to let her look upon him would be to invite trouble. She didn't remember him, and he needed to keep it that way, for both their sakes. The family he worked for, and their enemies, were always looking for a weakness to exploit. That was why he had done what he had needed to, and his more recent actions ensured she would never understand.

If their paths were to cross again, it would end only in misery and death.

CHAPTER 7

*L*eaving Maya, he descended the staircase, following the small hall to the dead end. Pressing his hand against the hallway wall, he exhaled, presenting his card to release the concealed mechanism. Magnets released a false wall like something straight out of an old movie. Fishing in his pocket he removed his wrought-iron key, another testament to his cousin's love of the old black-and-white pictures from beyond the barrier.

The key turned with a satisfying click, a hidden door opening inward to allow him entry into the cafe which occupied the ground floor of this building. The wall had been installed to stop the bedsit tenant doing exactly what he just had, but since the cafe was owned by his cousin, he was privy to all its secrets.

Raiden—since his hands had found their home on Maya's hips, he could no longer cling to the identity he had created in Blaze—lied when he told himself only the Thorne family knew of his existence. There were a few others who remembered him from before he had erased himself from sight and mind, and his cousin Lewis was one of them.

"Ray, you look like shit," Lewis called from behind the counter, tossing him a towel. They had a silent understanding. Raiden helped out with anything here that needed doing. That was what family did, they helped each other out. That's why he stayed in the bedsit, why he worked in the kitchens, out of sight, when he wasn't seeing to other business.

"Maya's upstairs."

"Fuck me, you actually did it, you actually brought her home?" Lewis had never met Maya, but Raiden had told him all about her. For the two to meet would put Lewis in harm's way. As far as anyone else was concerned Lewis was his landlord and employer, nothing more. But there was much more to their relationship, complexities that could not be voiced.

Lewis had taken him in the night he showed

up at the cafe a broken man, speaking of the deed he had done, of how he had purged himself from everyone's lives but the Thorne family's, and how he had ensured no one knew anything of her. Lewis had seen his pain, and from the look in his brown eyes, he wanted to know why he would subject himself to such heartbreak a second time. He ran his hand through his combed-back platinum blond hair, his intense stare seeking answers.

"Not like that, she was mugged. She almost risked her life for a damn bracelet. I just... I have to wait for her to leave."

"Want me to check on her?" He eyed his cousin cautiously. Unlike Raiden, Lewis was a pure-blood Thunderbird. Raiden, apparently, had the blood of Chione in his veins, allowing him to wield ice as well as lightning.

With his father and mother—or breeder, he didn't know which—being involved in a fatal accident while she was still pregnant, he never had the chance to ask any questions. He had been cut from her at the scene of the accident, given life when he should have died, and raised by his uncle.

He had discovered that while he was part Thunderbird, he could not embrace its form, merely use the element, just as he could call on snow and ice. His resulting blood had seen him classified as a member of the Celestial Clan, rather than the Initia Clan, like his uncle and cousin. "Since you fried her brain, it's not like she'd see any resemblance." Lewis slung his apron on the counter, waiting for the nod.

"I guess it would be unsettling for her to wake alone. I'll cover for you. Her things are in her purse. She's drunk." Things in the cafe were quiet at night, but Lewis insisted on remaining open to cover the clubbers and night workers, and to be fair, he did a good trade until about half-past one.

"You're not worried she'll seduce me? I mean, she fell for you, and we both know I got the looks." He paused, no doubt seeing Raiden's face drop, Lewis always teased him. He knew his cousin had only intended to lighten the mood, but where Maya was concerned, there'd never been any room for jokes. Some things felt more like a punch to the gut than a punchline. "Sorry, man. I know your story started once upon a time. I'll get her on her way safely." Raiden snatched the apron from his shoulder as Lewis left through the adjoining door.

Grabbing a washcloth, he began to wipe down the tables. His cousin was right. The day he'd met her, their fairytale had begun. For three years he had lived a dream. He had even started working nights so they could cuddle in bed and spend more of their between-shift time together. Three years ago, however, things changed, and he realised instead of a happily ever after, his life had been written as a tragedy, complete with star-crossed lovers and a tragic ending.

The problem was both his lives, old and new, had now become connected by one person, Maya. She was who his boss sought, she was who he had protected, and he didn't know how much longer he could hide the truth. That was the problem with lies and secrecy. Eventually the complex webs became unravelled.

By the time Raiden finished cleaning the tables his mind was in turmoil. One touch had undone the invisible wall he had erected between his past, where he was Raiden, in love and loved, and the present, where he was known as Blaze and was a fixer, of sorts, for the Thorne family. He had been working for this family since he was nineteen, since the day he had found himself within a prison cell with Zaz, one of their newest appraisers. He had been sentenced and sent to prison, but he only spent a few months there until the Thorne family intervened, and he found himself indebted to this family for more than just his freedom.

He'd met Maya a few years later. She was meant to be business, a way for the Thorne family to ensure her father wasn't getting any notions about talking. He'd had his motives too, all of which had gone straight out of the window when he had touched her. Just like tonight, she had been his unmaking each time their worlds crossed.

The small antique bell chimed above the cafe door. Without looking up Raiden grasped the mop and bucket, swilling the warm fluid across the floor. Lewis kept his cafe pristine, and maintaining this level of cleanliness had been drilled into him from the day he cooked his first meal in the kitchen.

"We're closing," he called, wringing out the mop before slapping it against the floor again.

"Perfect."

Raiden straightened at the sound of the voice, watching the man's slender fingers flip the sign to 'Closed' as he stepped inside, rotating the shuttered blind.

"Mr Thorne, what can I get for you, coffee?" Placing his mop to the wall, he gestured towards the kitchen.

"That treacle you serve here isn't coffee. This is a friendly visit. I noticed Johnathon Jameson is still on the prowl."

"Yes, sir, I have plans in motion for tomorrow. As things stand at present, there's too much security. I have it on good authority he's sneaking out to meet his mistress when his wife leaves for work in"—Raiden glanced at his watch—"a few hours."

"Whose authority?"

"My own. I used some of my connections to have a tap set on his device. They're meeting in a remote location, only he won't make it there." He may have also had someone mention to the mistress, in passing, that the wife was using the security detail to keep Jameson home and make sure their affair couldn't continue. The needy mistress fumed when the message had been relayed from one of his plants in the Finance Director's house. Especially when it was revealed the Jamesons' divorce had been put on hold while his wife tried to convince Johnathon a child would solve their problems. Especially since had promised to start a family with his mistress as soon as the divorce was finalised.

Raiden was good at having moving parts suitably greased and oiled in the places he predicted they would be of use in the future. He was a fixer for a reason. He saw the potential for problems before they even arose, and he handled people well. That, coupled with the fact he was the only person who knew who his contacts were —for their own safety as well as his—made him almost indispensable. Almost.

"Make sure he doesn't. I have another job for you too."

Raiden glanced at the boss's device and shook his head as he saw a contract on a young woman.

"I don't do women or children." It had been his one rule. He would do anything that needed to be done. He would achieve results, retrieve information, clean crime scenes, scrub anything digital, even make people disappear. His one line was that he would never bring harm to women or children, and he was so good at what he did, they had always respected his choice. He knew these things still happened, but it wasn't their blood on his own hands. It was the first time he had been asked to make an exception.

"Still sticking to your principles? It's one of the things I like about you, Blaze. No one else would dare tell to me no."

He wasn't sure if it was respect or warning in his tone.

"You certain you won't take a hit on a woman?"

Raiden didn't like the edge to his tone. It made his skin prickle uncomfortably. Before he opened his mouth to answer, Mr Thorne raised his hand. "Never mind. Just see that Johnathon Jameson, just like his newest policy and program, goes up in smoke. I need this fixing, Blaze. I need it fixed yesterday, and from what my intel reports, he belongs on one of your pyres."

Fuck. He knew. Yes, he had placed women on the pyres, but the situation had been different. He thought his boss understood that, maybe he'd seen more than he'd let on. It made Raiden wonder what else Thorne knew, if there had been another reason he was confirming the jobs he wouldn't take. Did he know about Maya? He resisted the urge to glance over his shoulder towards the door to the flat.

"By breakfast tomorrow neither will be a problem. The virus is already in place, it will trigger the moment his pulse flat-lines."

The bell chimed above the door a final time as Mr Thorne left. Without missing a beat, Raiden locked the door and finalised his plans. Everything would go down without a hitch, so why did he have a nagging feeling things were about to go horribly wrong? Was he right to read into that, had his deception been uncovered?

Maya took a deep breath, not daring to open her eyes. She felt the room still tilting around her, and at once cursed herself for drinking so much. She remembered everything that happened, right until the mugger struck her. She knew she should be terrified. She had been knocked unconscious, and could now feel the hard pressure of a mattress beneath her. But she found it hard to panic when the surrounding air was flooded with an aroma she hadn't smelled for too long, the crisp freshness of snow and winter winds.

Raiden's scent followed her from her dream, a dream in which they were intertwined in a dance of temptation. To open her eyes would be to release that final wisp of happiness. But there was a reason she should be alarmed, a reason to probe the darkness and look for a weapon. She knew this bed was not her own, that she had not somehow stumbled away from the attack in a drunken haze, if for no other reason than, whilst the mattress was as firm as the one in her bedroom, the rough scratching of the bobbled bedspread was unfamiliar against her touch.

"There she is." The voice grated in Maya's ears just seconds before she pushed herself upright. There was little point pretending; whoever watched over her recognised the moment she came around. "Easy there, miss, you're okay."

Maya checked herself mentally, her clothes were still intact, and whilst her jaw ached and her head throbbed in time with her pulse, there seemed no reason to scream, not that she felt the need to. That damn scent played with her survival instincts. How could she be in so much danger and still feel so safe? Her gaze travelled across the room to try to get her bearings.

The bed was small, a little larger than a standard single, meaning she would have to shuffle a little before her legs would hang over the edge. The rough blankets were grey, devoid of colour, much like the rest of the room. It was a dark place, small, made to feel more enclosed by the dreary paint. The grey had the slightest hint of blue, almost like the dark hue found in storm clouds, and stretched up the bare walls to capture the ceiling.

Beside her, on the bedside table, was a shadeless lamp and a bottle of water, the seal unbroken. To the left, an open door afforded her a glimpse into the tiny bathroom, and to her right was a wardrobe with a tarnished mirror mounted to its doors with brackets so dark they stood out against the pine-coloured wood.

The room was devoid of any personal touches except for a single star-shaped light catcher that dangled on an almost invisible thread from the shuttered skylight. Her heart quickened. She was in a room of storms and starlight, embraced by the crisp, clean scent of winter mornings. Raiden. Even now he haunted her thoughts.

She turned, sliding her legs from the bed, seeking the person who had beckoned her. She hadn't noticed it at first, the open door in the wall behind her to her right. It opened outward, the warm glow of light from outside spilling into the softly lit room. There the man stood, and, for the briefest moment, the shape of his eyes, the cut of his jaw, his frame, all reminded her of Raiden. But it wasn't him. Her stomach knotted with a burn beyond that which was caused by the copious amounts of alcohol she'd consumed. His hair platinum hair was slicked back, making his analysing brown eyes seem darker against his tanned complexion. He seemed to frown as he studied her, his pale eyebrows drawing together, as if he'd read the disappointment in her expression.

"Where am I?" she questioned, flinching as the strange man approached, passing her the water from the small table. The room was tiny, too small to be sharing with a stranger. He grabbed something from the table, a piece of paper, screwing it up before tossing it into the empty waste-bin in the corner. Maya let her vision linger on the bottle under the pretence of checking the seal to prevent herself from looking at him again.

"You were mugged just outside. Thought it was better you woke up somewhere safe. Your things are in your purse by the way." But Maya didn't glance towards where he gestured, instead her fingers went to her wrist, alarm flooding through her. She had been in the process of fastening her bracelet when the mugger cornered her. She grasped her purse desperately, spilling its contents across the bedspread. The dull sound of coins striking the floor barely registered as she hastily spread the contents out until she caught the familiar glint. Her fingers curled around the bracelet, clutching it to her chest as she heaved out a relieved sigh.

"Thank you." There was no small measure of awkwardness in her voice as she shoved her belongings back into her purse, ignoring the coins claimed by gravity. Pushing herself up, she felt herself blush as the man made no attempt to disguise the way his gaze examined her from head to toe with an approving nod. "I should be on my way, thank you...erm..."

"Lewis." He took the hand she awkwardly extended and gave it a shake before he stepped aside, granting her unrestricted access to the door. "If you want to wait for the Blue Coats, I can give them a call. We've a camera out back, so it could help them find whoever jumped you."

"Thanks, I appreciate it. It was my own fault, I don't normally drink." She tucked her tangled locks behind her ear self-consciously.

"So why were you?"

"Ghosts of the past," she whispered, her embarrassed gaze fixed on the bracelet's clasp as she tried and failed to secure it. She felt his strong hands still her attempts. She stiffened as he lifted the chain from her grasp, securing it around her wrist. He seemed to study it for a moment before releasing her.

"Well, hopefully your spirits chased them away." He made a gesture like he was knocking back a shot, just in case she missed his pun, the action itself more amusing than his terrible joke. "But you being vulnerable is no excuse for someone to take advantage. You sure you're okay to get home from here, I can call a cab."

"That's sweet but," she studied him again, the throbbing in her head clearing just a fraction, enough for her to feel the electricity in the air warming her bracelet, "the taxi rank is just at the other end of the entry."

"I could escort you. You still look a little unsteady."

"Thank you, but I'll be okay." She took another sip of water from the bottle, feeling strangely sober despite her body still warning her of intoxication.

"Right. Well, if you change your mind and need a witness, you know where to find me. I'll save the footage."

"I, erm, thanks. Not a lot of people would help someone." There it was, the flood of awkwardness she expected. It took long enough for her mind and body to remember she was in a stranger's home, a stranger who had dragged her from the streets and seemingly wanted nothing in return.

"You're right about that, Maya-m." She stiffened for a moment before realising he had called her ma'am, not Maya. She saw him glance over his shoulder as she reached the open door before angling his body to watch her leave. She lowered her head, hurrying past, down the stone stairs away from the awkward exchange.

As she reached the external door, she turned back, watching him close the door to the bedsit. She glanced at her bracelet where visible sparks now seemed to dance upon its surface, just like they had when Raiden had placed it in her hand that night in the mountains.

She paused for a moment. She wanted to think on this bizarre reaction, but her head pounded, her arms ached, and all she wanted to do was get home. Her hand hesitated upon the door before pulling it open. She would think about it later. Home, shower, sleep. That was what she needed now.

CHAPTER 8

*A*shley rolled to the side, more strands of her rust-coloured hair breaking free of their bindings as she evaded the weapon. She struck the ground too hard, tucking as soon as she realised what was happening, but not before she felt the force of the floor. Even with her momentum, she hadn't moved quickly enough. The sting of the weapon burnt her back, bringing tears to her eyes. She struggled to her knees, turning to face her attacker who watched her with a bemused smirk.

Her brother, Alex, looked down on her, shaking his head before extending his hand. She grasped it firmly, feeling how cool his skin was compared to her clammy grasp. He had been doing this for years, something apparent by the fact he hadn't even broken a sweat. "You watch too many films, what possessed you to roll?" Alex was a great looking man. It made her feel bad that only a handful of people got to see what he really looked like under the constant glamour his frost bird essence portrayed. He appeared slightly different to everyone. Even members of his own team had no idea what he looked like under the seamless distortion. That was the price he paid for his undercover work. He was often stationed beyond the barrier, and to be outed as a member of the P.T.F. would mean death.

"How many times do I have to tell you? Practical not fancy. Never show an enemy your back."

"It wasn't so much a roll as falling with grace," she panted. She had intended to pivot, sidestep, or jump back—she knew all the ways she *should* have avoided that attack—but instead, she tried to execute all three simultaneously, lost her balance, and ended up tripping over her own feet.

"Trust me, sis, there was *nothing* graceful about that. You need to get out of your own head, react instead of over-think."

She knew Alex was between missions at the moment, which meant he was pouring every free moment in trying to get her, his baby sister, ready for some unknown feat. Just last spring, she had been caught up in a dark situation and had discovered not only the truth of her origin, but that soul mates were something more than a fable. Alex's parents had adopted her when she was a young girl and ensured no one could discover her secret until she could be protected. She was a Perennial, a being thought to be extinct. But it seemed more were awakening and finding their way here as if driven by fate.

At twenty-one, she was the youngest in this compound, a baby to everyone. Even the newest recruits, those selected from the rigorous P.T.F. training program, were twenty-three, having already dedicated three years to training and studies in the hope of finishing in the top three percent of their team. But Ashley had a place reserved for her she hadn't even known about, put into place the moment she had been adopted.

Of all her family, only she had not known what she was, and that was because all her abilities had been suppressed for her protection. She hated thinking she was getting an easy ride, Perennials were rare, and she was enlisted straight into the ranks. She trained as hard as she worked, intent on proving to everyone she deserved this place as much as they did. That included extra training with her brother who, for the moment at least, dedicated his free time to this new unit.

Just a few months ago Jesse had joined them, a druid who could control the souls of shifters and nature spirits. It had started with Ashley, but the P.T.F. were assembling a new task force, one which would be in place to staunch the uprising that seemed to be moving in the shadows in a power-play to overthrow the council who governed Mython. Part of their plan, it seemed, involved spreading a new virus, known as Pyrexia Blight—or PB for short—which recent intelligence revealed was actually a discrete way of creating an army. There were many units in training for such things, but Ashley's unit was special. Although the details had yet to be disclosed, Alex had simply said they would be pivotal to preventing the coming war.

Ashley's abilities could destroy the infection in a host, but as yet, no way had been discovered to create a vaccine. She was a phoenix, and her saliva burnt away the disease. But she was just one person, and the only person she wanted to kiss was Conrad. Her burning hot ifrit. Besides, it wasn't as if she could go around kissing everyone who drew breath.

The best she had accomplished was introducing her saliva to hot chocolate, a trick she had used at Overton Academy, but even then it had only stretched as far as her small class. She was glad the P.T.F. had allowed her to finish her studies remotely after being taken into their custody. It seemed she had always been destined to wind up here, although training and working alongside her brother was something which wouldn't become commonplace. He had his own life, his own missions, and they all existed beyond the barrier.

"So you say. Let's go again." She broke free of her thoughts, surprised her brother hadn't taken advantage of her distraction to deliver another blow.

"Actually, I've something else in mind. I've put Conrad under Captain Hayes, for the time being. I think he'll benefit from his skills. For the next hour I'd like you to train with Jesse, see if she can wrestle control from you, but don't resist her, she needs to get a feel for this, and she trusts you."

"Sure." Ashley's easy smile lit up her face, causing her smoky grey eyes to sparkle. She liked Jesse. She had arrived at the Preternatural Taskforce—P.T.F.—headquarters a few months ago after single-handedly taking down her father, the Lord of Windmere, and releasing the familiars he had bound in servitude. This single act dealt a devastating blow to the forces attempting to rally against the council, and since then, the number of people newly afflicted with PB slowed.

It was nice to have another female around. Jesse was finally starting to relax around her, and Ashley hadn't needed to see her scars to know her life had been anything but easy.

"Alpha Ciele, we have a detective Mendel on the line." Ashley felt the mat on her back as the air was expelled from her lungs. Alex looked at her with a mischievous smile, spinning the quarterstaff cockily.

"Patch him through." Alex nodded towards the woman now standing at the training room's door, plucking his device from the floor where their water bottles had been deposited. "Hey, detective, what can I do for you?" Ashley stayed silent, wanting to hear what had been so important that her boyfriend's father had felt it necessary to place a call. No matter how hard she strained her hearing, she could only hear her brother's side of the conversation. "Well, our normal healer is on assignment, but I can have Will and Ashley take a look. How far are they from base?"

~

Will ruffled a hand through his golden hair, making it appear messier than the tousled look he normally wore. He had avoided Ashley as much as possible since he had awoken with her at his bedside. The look of betrayal she levelled towards him had softened over the last few weeks, but she still didn't trust him, not completely. Not that he could blame her. It made him wonder why she had pulled him from his coma at all. He hadn't deserved her mercy, but had to admit he was grateful for it.

What he had done to her was inexcusable, and if not for his later actions of saving one of her childhood friends, Jack, he was certain she would have left him to rot. As far as everyone had been concerned, he had burnt out his energy while trying to keep Jack in the land of the living, causing massive internal damage to both his energy systems and his body. He had lain in a coma for three months before she tiptoed into his room one night.

He would never confess to it, but he remembered her every word as she dribbled her blood into his mouth. She had told him what he had done was unforgivable, that he was the reason she had been abducted and almost sold as a breeder. She had vented her frustrations on him in whispers, ensuring she would not be found by the staff nursing him. She spoke of the betrayal, how his actions hurt her. She told him everything, gaining closure for herself as she bared his worst and most shameful actions, actions he wished he could erase.

Her voice had grown even quieter as she told him she had to forgive him because, while it had been his fault she was taken, he was also the reason Jack was alive and she had been found, and because of that, and the fact his gran had already lost her only child and deserved more than a life of pain and sadness, she would do this. She would balance their scales of debt. But if he ever so much as laid a hand on her again, she would not hesitate to kill him.

Her words had been for her alone. She had no way to know he heard every conversation since slipping into a coma, and so he kept what he knew to himself. When his eyes opened, she stood over him, venom in her gaze. Without a word, she had left. He had avoided her since, not sure how to earn the forgiveness she seemed to think herself capable of. This was the first time he could not duck away when he caught sight of her. It was time to face his demon.

He knocked on the training room door,

where Ashley stood bathed in vibrant orange flames. The way they danced across her molten skin was hypnotic. Her entire body forged of fire. But she was only allowing the barest taste of her power to emerge as she tried to help Jesse understand the feeling of her soul. Jesse was improving, which he was grateful for. It meant Captain Hayes no longer stole to his room in the night while she was sleeping, asking if he could heal her burns. Right now, fire danced on Jesse's fingertips, her face contorted in concentration as sweat glistening upon her brow.

When Will heard the Lady of Windmere was joining Ashley's small squadron, he'd expected an entitled snob. Not a woman who could only portray confidence for so long as you weren't standing too close. There was a look of elation on Jesse's face, her blue eyes sparkling with a rare genuine smile often not seen outside Captain Hayes' presence. This task seemed to be a harder process than dominating a shifter. He had seen her do that with some semblance of fluidity. He felt almost guilty at having to knock, to disturb this moment of small triumph, but their task was not one which could wait.

The flames dissipated as his knock sounded. Ashely had mastered her phoenix well, her yoga pants and tank top no longer steamed or scorched when she pulled the fiery essence back into herself. Unlike shifters, who possessed one vessel for two souls, altering their shape to the dominant essence, elementals did not change their form. Their essence simply bled from them, building a new body upon their old like a protective shield that was still every bit a part of them as their flesh and blood protected beneath.

"Great job, Jesse," Ashley encouraged as Jesse pulled her blonde hair from her loose ponytail, before securing it again, tighter. "You're getting better." She said something else as she handed Jesse a towel, something Will didn't quite catch, but knowing Ashley, it would be aimed at helping her. That was the thing about Ashley; she loved and encouraged everyone. It was her personal mission in life to elevate them, which was another reason what he had done to her had been so repulsive.

"It's not easy. I don't know if I can do this. Shifters are one thing, they stand apart making the energy easy to control, but you, what you are is in your own soul, not separate."

"You've got this, trust me. You're making amazing progress. See? Not a mark." Ashley took Jesse's hand in hers, tracing her fingers. The finch was minimal, the tension almost invisible. She tolerated the touch, her demeanour so different than how she was with everyone else.

Ashley's warm smile cooled as she turned towards him, and he could tell she tried to keep the chill from her glare for no other reason than to keep Jesse at ease. As their eyes met, her gaze softened, just a fraction. "Are they here?"

Not wanting to risk further complicating their strained relationship, he simply nodded, leading the way towards the P.T.F. medical ward. The wards here were not too different to those found in the hospital. Truth be told, their layout was identical. There wasn't much more you could do with a bed and a bathroom to make it appear unique. One thing that was different, however, threaded through the soft white tiles, woven throughout each room, was a special conductor that, when activated, prevented the use of preternatural abilities, much like the suppressor charms on the handcuffs carried by the Blue Coats.

"Ashley, Will," Alex acknowledged as they approached the room he hovered outside. It seemed whoever had brought this person in had made a hasty retreat. There was no sign of anyone. In fact, no one at all seemed to be around, as if the floor had been cleared for them.

"He's in there." Alex inclined his head towards the closed metal door.

"What do we know?" Will asked. He chanced a glance towards Ashley, still not understanding why both of them would be summoned for the same person. He was a healer, competent in healing a wide range of injuries. Ashley, however, was something completely different. He wasn't quite sure the scope of her skills and knew better than to make enquiries. From what he could tell she couldn't heal physical wounds, yet she could purge sickness from the blood, replenish energy, and, well the truth was, he had no idea what it had taken to heal him, but he knew from experience her blood had raised his own blood count and purity.

"His name's Fredrick McArther, 46. He suffered a cardiac incident about a week ago and was resuscitated on site. Today he was involved in a workplace accident, scaffolding collapsed, resulting in two broken ribs and a broken arm, but that's not the worst of it. One of the tubes pierced his chest. He was cut free at the scene, and after speaking to Reuben, I arranged for him to be transported here."

"Why here?"

"Let's go take a look." Alex opened the door, extending his arm to allow them entry.

Sitting in the chair next to the crisply made bed, gazing out of the window, was a very pale man, his black hair caked with the same sweat, dust, and blood that covered his clothes and skin. Biting back a question of, *what the hell*, Will approached, his gaze gravitating to the inches of pipe that protruded from the man's chest.

He felt his stomach clench. Nothing could have prepared him for this.

To push back the bile rising in his throat, he focused on the small details first. The tube was galvanised steel of three-inch diameter. The edges were rough from the cuts made by the first responders, leaving a length protruding from his torso where it impaled, directly through his heart. Will swallowed again. Yep, he could see the strong pulses moving the metal with each beat of his heart, a beep punctuated with the bleeping of one of the many monitors synchronised to the man's chip.

He leaned closer, all too aware his temperature plummeted as, between the damaged muscle and drying blood, he swore he could see the slightest hint of light. The pipe hadn't just perforated one of the man's most integral organs; it had passed straight through him.

"Hello, Mr McArther." Will's voice wavered

slightly as he made himself stand tall and stop staring.

"Bit of a mess, aren't I?" The man chuckled. The man, with a tube straight through his heart, actually chuckled before somehow raising his broken arm, as if he had nothing more than a slight ache. He felt Fredric McArther's rough skin, calloused from years of manual labour, slide across his own before grasping his hand with a strength that defied belief.

This man was a miracle, alive with a fatal injury, his heart still beating around the metal tube, and yet, as Will continued to hold his hand, he knew that this was no miracle.

The man before him possessed no life energy.

He was dead.

He was sitting there, in a chair, talking about how terrible his day had been, recounting tales of the accident that should have killed him, but he was already dead.

Will tried his best not to stumble as he backed away towards the door. He was dead, a talking corpse who seemed to think he was still alive. Dead.

"You okay there, Will?" He hadn't realised he'd backed out of the door, or that Alex and

Ashley both followed his retreat until he was propped up by the nurses' station.

"The tubing... it goes right through his..." Will whispered, his voice failing before he could finish his sentence.

"Straight through his heart," Alex confirmed.

"You sure he's not, I don't know, incorporeal?" Will's voice sounded, strangled to his ears. He must have looked worse than he felt because Ashley placed her hand on his arm. It was only then he realised at some point, despite the support at his back, he was sitting on the floor. He felt like every ounce of energy had been stripped from him, and his body only now realised it.

"Talk to me," she whispered. He didn't miss the tenderness in her voice. He must really look like crap. But he couldn't process what he'd just seen, what he'd felt. The lack of life energy assaulted him with its wrongness; he could still feel the perversion of everything that made someone alive.

He couldn't find the thoughts, the words, it just felt wrong, dark and wrong. His body shook, haunted by the complete void. He pushed his hands through his hair, his body trembling beyond his control. His mind twisted in darkness as if his soul descended into the twisting bowels of hell itself.

"He's dead." Will forced the words through chattering teeth. "He's dead and—" Another shudder wracked him.

"Lex, I think he's going into shock." He heard someone say, was that still Ashley? People moved around him, leaving echoes of their figures that fought to catch up to their moving bodies. The next thing he knew, there was a blanket around his shoulders.

"He's not just dead." Will wondered when Conrad had arrived; he stood behind Ashley, wrapping his arms around her waist as he pulled her towards him, placing a gentle kiss on her cheek. It was the last thing he saw before darkness swallowed his vision. He wasn't unconscious. He was blinded by the dark motes swimming across his vision. "He's tethered. If the healer's touched him, I'm surprised he's still conscious." Conrad no longer referred to Will by name, not after discovering what he had done.

"Conrad, what brought you here?" That distorted voice was Alex's, he was certain of it. A small amount of the haze began to clear, his body's healing energy trying to find an equilibrium.

"He's unnatural, I could hear him before he even reached the complex. Who sent him here?"

"Your father," Alex answered. Will blinked, trying to dispel the blots dancing before his gaze, relieved when small fragments began to return.

"He didn't warn you?"

"He didn't have eyes on the scene. He thought the victim may need protection; he's part of an ongoing investigation. You've heard of the serial killer Pyre-starter." People must have nodded because Alex continued. "Detective Mendel thinks he's choosing his victims based on the patients of a certain medic. He was one of hers."

"So you think the construction accident was deliberate?" Ashley questioned. Will could see clearly enough now to follow her gaze to closed door, her hands cupping her mouth.

"No, I think it really was an accident. What do you mean, he's tethered?" Alex questioned, now perched against the nurses' station.

"His soul, it's tethered between his body and the underworld."

"How?"

"I don't know."

"Necromancers," Will offered, his voice sounding stronger than before. "You know, from those old movies beyond the barrier, they bring the dead back to life. That would explain why touching him depleted me, they're like the anti-healer."

"There's no such thing as—" Ashley began.

"But there used to be. They were called reapers," Alex offered. "Many of the old stories from that world have a foot in ours. Reapers were a class of Perennial who could do what Jesse does, but to the undead. They guide and command souls of the deceased and control the bodies of the dead. So how do we relieve him of his suffering?" Alex turned to Conrad, whose gaze turned to Ashley with a hint of regret.

"A kiss?" Ashley questioned.

"That's messed up," Will whispered as Ashley entered the room, but both Alex and Conrad ignored him. "So if we've got a reaper on our hands, why are they raising an undead army? It's not as if a construction worker has any real influence. What are we looking at here?"

"That's what we need to uncover. I think I'll start by asking Detective Mendel about his investigations. We may just have uncovered something useful. I don't think the Pyre-starter is a serial killer, I think they're remedying the situation. The real question is, if Pyre-starter ends up being the solution, who is the cause?"

CHAPTER 9

Maya groaned, pulling her pillow closer as she tried to resist the sound dragging her from slumber. The soft chime had only sounded for a few seconds, and she already knew she would answer it, hangover or not. She programed her device to silent mode when she was asleep.

The only call able to bypass this, as per her settings, was the hospital. She buried her face into her pillow and groaned, reaching across the varnished nightstand, muttering a curse as she heard the loud thump of her water bottle hit the plush carpet. Finally, with the device in her grasp, she rolled over, accepting the call, already knowing how it would go. She squinted against the evening sun streaming through the open curtains. Her bedroom was a corner room with two windows, two points of entry for the sun's rays to assault her tender eyes and increase the throbbing in her head.

"Hello," she whispered. The moment her mouth moved, she was reminded of the bruise by the tight and sore feeling of her skin.

"Sorry to wake you, Bambi. We need a favour, any chance you can cover tonight?" It was her S.O., and she could tell by the strain in his voice calling her had been his final option.

"Sure," she mumbled, turning back towards the door. Her stomach churned when she saw it was ajar. Whenever she slept in this room, she always locked it. Then again, she had been a mess, stumbling through the house half-drunk, and vomiting several times in the toilet, before collapsing on her bed in tears. Yes, there had been tears, as the dampness on her pillow reminded her.

"You're a lifesaver," came the voice of the S.O. as she tried without joy to find a place to lay her head that was a little drier.

"Is Davey okay?"

"Yeah, he needed a few more days with his family." The slight edge to Station Officer Silvers' voice instantly cast aside any doubt that he viewed all of his team as family; he genuinely cared about what his teams were going through.

"Tell him to get back whenever he's ready. I know what losing a parent can do to you. I'm glad he was able to be there when... you know, it helps. I'll keep taking his shifts until he's ready to come back."

"You sure? You're meant to be off after that stretch you just pulled." Twenty-eight days. It wasn't her record, but it was still enough to hear the worry in the station officer's voice. For him to call her this evening meant he had already tried the others who would cover, but most of them had families. She was alone, she had no one to stay home for, and even when she was with Rick, she found his attitude made her want to spend more time away than in his company.

"That's the best part about us working rotas, I can cover his four with my off."

"Bambi, since when have you worked four-on-four-off?"

"I don't know boss, I think there was a time when I first transferred over," she teased, feeling more awake.

"You're too good to us, you know. I already have cover for Thursday, but how do you feel about tonight and tomorrow and Friday?"

"Fine by me. It's not like I have anything else

going on, sir. I'll see you at seven. Oh, by the way, next month I have to get my surgery signed off. Can I get some time off? Doctor Gilbert is going to arrange a few night shifts for us and get the boxes ticked." Hospital policy was that any qualified surgeon who was not actively practising had to have a set number of observed surgeries, both in the theatre and on dummies, signed off every four to six months. Not doing this would mean she had to take a refresher course should she ever want to return to the field. As she had already proven, her training saved lives, and even though she had given her career up for Raiden, she refused to lose her skills. She lamented her decision after the incident with Jameson, wondering if she could somehow do both. She had even been drafting a mental proposal letter, right until those hands had found her hips and hit the mental delete button.

"Bambi, that's on the clock time. Just let me know when and I'll make sure you're covered."

"Thanks, sir."

"And speaking of time, when are you planning to take your vacations? With all your extra work, you've earned quite a substantial amount." Holiday pay worked the same no matter what job you worked: hours worked were counted towards holiday, so overtime and shift covering also resulted in additional holiday pay. An employee could choose to have them bought from them, resulting in a tax-free payment, or take them as leave. Often Maya used half of her holidays during the year and had the others purchased back. This year, however, had been a difficult one. Her normal time off over the anniversary of her father's death had been withdrawn when Davey had discovered his mother had cancer. He had gone to spend her last days with her, planning to return after the funeral, and without even a pause for thought, Maya had cancelled her leave and picked up most of his shifts.

"Don't worry, chief, I'll be sure to get some of them booked."

"Oh, circling back to what you said about surgical." There was a pregnant silence, long enough for Maya to wonder if she had been speaking aloud her deepest thoughts in her hung-over stupor. "The chief of surgery put a call through yesterday. It seems the video of you operating on that financial director caught a lot of attention. He wants to know if you'd be interested in a little work on the side, to fit in with you."

"What's he thinking?" Maya sat up, instantly

regretting the decision as the pounding in her head worsened.

"One extra day, at the end of your four-on."

"Is he serious?" This was almost what she had been planning to propose. Being alone, she didn't need all this time off, she didn't need to rattle around her house. Charlie Gilbert must have seen the look in her eyes, the one that stated quite passionately that she may have moved away from surgery, but she was nowhere near finished with it.

"Bambi, you're a damn good trauma surgeon. I've been getting heat ever since you came over to send you back. If it's something you want, I won't object, we'll make it work. I watched the video, the way you took control of that situation, how effortless you made it look. You were born to do that. As much as I hate to say it, your skills are wasted here."

"Chief, my skills are just fine where they are. If I hadn't been on scene, Mr Jameson would have bled out before anyone could have attended. I'll think over the offer, five-on-three-off sounds quite appealing, and it'll mean I don't have to keep taking time out to do the observed surgery. Thanks, sir. Anyway, I better go get some breakfast. See you later." With that she terminated the called, placing her device back on her bedside table.

Maybe she could have both after all. When she was thinking about it, it seemed ludicrous they would accept such a deal, but now, here Charlie was, suggesting it himself. She'd joined the medics in the hope of using their broader resources to locate Raiden. She loved the job, but nothing compared to the feeling of cutting into someone and fixing them from the inside out.

She closed her eyes. She wouldn't remind herself of all the things she missed, quite simply because the strength of those emotions were nothing compared to how she felt without Raiden, and she still wasn't willing to give up looking for him. Not yet. Not now. Not ever.

Wrestling with the covers, she stripped the bed, cramming the bedding into the washing machine before peeling last night's clothes from her and hopping into the shower.

A squeal echoed around the wet room as the steaming water turned ice cold, icy jets sending shampoo into her open mouth as she slipped, grabbing the rail just in time to stop her tumbling to the floor. Her arm screamed in agony under the extra strain of suddenly supporting her weight as she tried to dodge from the icy caress.

Damn washing machine, she cursed.

One day she would see to the plumbing, but for now, there was little choice but to resign herself to the game of water roulette. She'd become fairly skilled at it over the years and, if nothing else, the game woke her up, although did little for her pounding head.

Maya's shift passed like most others, nothing overly terrible happened, so she and Oliver—the person who normally partnered with Davey—managed to spend a few hours at the station between calls, restocking their supplies, cleaning their vehicle, and catching up on reports. There was even time to start a movie and sit down to a hot takeaway. Maya politely declined, sticking to a few bites of dry toast while her tender stomach complained at even the thought of food after last night's drinking.

Normally they averaged around twenty call-outs during the night shift, which meant the two night-shift ambulances were always on the move. But tonight—aside from a few minor accidents and a bar brawl—it had been quiet. The two teams answered only five call-outs between them. Maya always thought of times like these as the calm before a storm. Without fail, the universe always made sure to catch up.

After showering at the station and slipping back into her clothes, Maya's stomach finally told her it was time to put something more than just a dried piece of toast and an energy bar in her stomach. Deciding to leave her car on the car park and do a little shopping, she let the crisp morning air wash over her, feeling the way it bit into her damp scalp as she made the short walk towards the town centre.

The trees lining the busy roads were awash in autumn shades. The sun hung low in the sky, which was the soft shade of blue that came with the season. It was doubtful to be visible for long if the thin clouds rolling in were anything to go by, but the morning was pleasant, crisp and colourful. Something about the air at this time of year captured the scents from the nearby cafes that were already a few hours into their day, seeing to their morning patrons who ordered breakfast while Maya was on the hunt for her tea. She chuckled to herself. Only people who worked nights understood that the meal other people called breakfast was in fact tea for the night owls.

A sharp sting at her wrist had her batting away an imaginary wasp before she realised the tingling sensation spreading across her skin came from her bracelet. Looking to it, her brow furrowed, noticing how the graphite started to heat against her flesh. With each step she took, it seemed to grow hotter. With a slight shrug, she committed herself to unlocking this secret.

Since last night it felt as if her bracelet had become possessed, shocking her, growing warm, even sparking. As much as she felt a fool weaving in and out of open shops and peering through windows of closed boutiques, she was determined to find out what caused this bizarre occurrence. She had convinced herself that the last time she thought she'd felt its heat, seen these sparks, it had been nothing more than a vision caused by her alcohol-riddled mind.

Thinking back, she recalled all the times it had seemed to grow warm against her wrist before, but nothing like this, nothing like the other night. This was just bizarre, and if she wasn't so infatuated, she may have been afraid. She undid the clasp, holding it tightly in her palm, waiting to see if the sensation altered.

The graphite felt as though it was charged, sticking to her skin like a magnet while lashing out at her with tiny jolts of electricity. She couldn't explain any of it. As she stopped before a café, she felt the soft sting of sparks against her flesh increase. It wasn't a painful sensation. In fact, as she closed her eyes, it seemed almost on par with a soft touch. Pulling the stone from her finger, she saw the tendrils of lightning between herself and it.

She shook her head, staring at it for a moment as she wondered if this was it. If this was the moment she lost the last scrap of her sanity. Perhaps her old friends had been right, perhaps it had been a mental break, and now it was coming to a head. But still, she couldn't tear her gaze away.

In for a penny in for a pound.

She froze at the doorway, the handle still clutched in her grasp as the small bell above the door announced her presence. She recognised the man behind the counter; he was the same man who had caused her bracelet to spark just the night before. So it was him, something about the graphite responded to him, but why? She stepped inside, allowing the door to fall closed. She was going to speak with him, seek an answer she wasn't even sure he could provide, but before she could offer him a smile, her gaze diverted to the only other person in the cafe.

Breathe.

Her heart felt as if it was about to stop, and the breath did not come. He wore a dark hoodie, his gaze turned down towards his device, but there was no denying who it was. It took her more than a second to remember to actually pull a breath into her lungs, the result a tiny gasp upon her lips.

Breathe.

He sat in the shadows, but she knew it was him. Walking through this door, being assailed with the fragrance of strong coffee and toast had not diminished his scent or the way the air between them seemed somehow charged, as if it drew everything she was towards him with a force she was powerless to resist.

She began to walk to the counter in a daze. It was better than standing there staring. Her heart, once intent on stopping, began to race, telling her to do something, but her mind scrambled. After all these years, after all this time, there he was. Raiden. Sitting in a café of all places, living his life, acting as if nothing had happened.

Why hadn't he glanced up? Couldn't he feel the charge, the energy drawing them towards one another? He was a magnet, and she the metal trapped in his pull, unable to resist. She walked past him, feeling her shoulders stiffen as the crisp fragrance of winter mornings invited her to take a seat. Her heart hammered as she stepped past his booth, but her feet would carry her no further.

Raiden was here, in the café, and he hadn't even glanced towards her.

The small bell above the door chimed, drawing Raiden's focus from the task at hand for just long enough to know he shouldn't be looking. Long enough for him to slide down just a little further in the corner of his booth using the partition to push his hood further forward. News of Johnathon Jameson's death was just breaking as reporters flocked to the scene of his latest pyre where the victim had already been identified.

It had taken them less than twenty-four hours to find this latest corpse, but subtlety was so far out the window now that its reflection was not even a glimmer on the horizon. He had been waiting for this story over a mug of bitter coffee, while double-checking that his virus had scrubbed all of Jameson's software development from any system its coding had ever touched. He told himself he was being thorough by sitting up checking everything had been completed without a hitch, but he knew it was just an excuse not to go back to his room, to the place where he could still smell Maya when he lay on his bed. The last thing he had expected in that moment was for her to walk through the door.

She stood bathed in the light of the morning sun, her damp hair tied back, dressed in leggings and a loose t-shirt suggesting she had just left work. He felt himself frown. When last he'd checked, her rota she should have been off. Something must have changed. Which meant he had a night's worth of playing catch up to do. He kept his head down, his attention glued to the screen of his device while he watched her walk past in his peripheral vision.

Last night had not been a good night. The order had come in telling him to report for a status update, not for the Jameson task, which his boss was content had been handled, but the other assignment, the one he had been delaying. They were getting restless. Since he had failed to find the reaper himself, Zaz was being called in, and if that was the case, it would be only a matter of time until Maya was discovered. A reaper, he still couldn't believe it, but he had seen her gift with his own eyes.

If there was one thing he knew for certain, it was that he couldn't let the Thorne family get their hands on her. They were the greater evil. He knew of another option, a place where she might have a chance, but he wasn't sure he trusted them with her safety either.

Perennials were meant to be extinct, they sacrificed their lives to erect the barrier and set the world beyond the barrier to rights. They were extinct, which made Maya dangerous. She possessed an old power, was walking proof things were changing. She had no idea what she was doing. It made her vulnerable, unable to defend herself against those who would come for her. They would break her, bind her into servitude. The woman he loved would not survive if his boss was ever to get his hands upon her. Maya would not survive being broken, and Mython would not survive a broken reaper.

He watched the slight change in her posture as she walked past, the way her shoulders seemed to stiffen ever so slightly as her shoe skimmed the floor with a step not fully measured.

She didn't know him, wouldn't recognise the face she had once studied as he slept, but he knew better than to linger. He had been a fool before, giving in to the temptation of being close to her as their song seduced, taking him to a time where his hands upon her had been the most natural thing. Now the cravings he fought for so long were raw. There was no denying he was addicted to her. He couldn't let her go, yet he couldn't have her either.

As soon as she was past the low partition, he slipped his device into his pocket. Scooting across the seat, he stood to leave. But his feet wouldn't move. She stood before him, their chests barely inches apart as she barred his retreat. Her eyes were on his face, searching desperately for something as her lips parted.

"Excuse me," he muttered, trying to edge around her to step from the booth. He avoided reaching out, touching her shoulders to move her aside. Instead, he pressed himself painfully close to the table as he edged around, trying to dismiss the pull, the way his body seemed to want to press against hers to feel the sparks that sang between them.

Free from the booth, he lowered his head, shoving his hands into his pocket as he turned away. Her boots invaded his field of vision as she sidestepped, blocking his path once more. Her hands were on his shoulders, her movements so quick his only reaction had been to flinch backwards as she pressed her soft lips to his. Her grip tightened, holding him in place as she kissed him again, her tongue teasing his lips, seeking to gain entrance while her fingers traced up his jaw until she pushed his hood down.

"Storms and starlight," she breathed, her breath tickling his still closed lips. He saw the shimmer of tears as she kissed him more desperately. Her hands wove in his hair, preventing him from pulling back as he used every ounce of his willpower to remain passive, to not respond to something he had craved to feel so desperately for three years. He closed his eyes, letting her tongue part his lips, allowing himself another moment of sin before he raised his arms to ease her away, or at least that had been his intention. "Raiden," she moaned, tightening her grip.

His name on her lips was his undoing. His fingers released her hair from the scrunchy, weaving within the cold, damp locks as he crushed his lips to hers, kissing her back, matching her passion, her desperation with every flick of his tongue as he claimed her mouth, making it his once more.

She remembered him.

He had thought the way she had moved on the dance floor was a coincidence, but she knew him, recognised him. The realisation stole his breath as much as the kiss they shared. But it was more than a kiss, more than the crashing of lips, it was coming home, it was his heart beginning to beat, it was the very essence of his life being returned. It was complete and utter destruction, and for her, he would gladly crumble.

His arm slipped around her waist, pulling her body into his, removing the offending space that dared come between them. He had felt every moment they had been apart, every inch that separated them, and lived with the heartbreak of watching her in someone else's arms. All of it crashed over him as he sought to claim her. Pulling away he trailed kisses down her neck, hearing her moan, a serenade somewhere between pleasure and heartbreak.

Enough was enough.

This game was over.

She was his.

He couldn't do this any longer, he couldn't watch her from afar, not now she had captured him with her spell. She possessed no power over the living, but without her, part of him had died. Even though his heart kept beating, his name upon her lips captured him, bending him to her will. He would serve her willingly to the end of his life. Then he would protect her from the grave. She had always possessed him, he had always been hers. His mind raced as his lips sought hers again, her weight supported by his arm as her knees went weak.

He could do what he needed to and still be

beside her. How else could he protect her from what was to come?

"Why did you leave me?" she whispered through tears as he cast a glance towards Lewis, who stood awkwardly at the counter, seemingly unable to tear his gaze away from their reunion. He gave a nod, opening the adjoining door to the flat above, the one she would recognise as the place she woke after that thug had dared lay his hand upon her. The flat opened at the back of the building, keeping the two properties separate if not for the hidden door.

"You remember me," he whispered. It was no longer a question. "How did you find me?"

She pulled away from him just long enough to reveal the bracelet she had almost lost her life protecting. This time, however, he saw it was not just her mother's chain. He could see the small tendrils of plasma dancing around a carefully mounted stone.

He froze, recognising it. He had given her a piece of graphite on their third date, promising to one day trade it for a diamond. It had been a spur of the moment gesture. He had spotted the stone during their nighttime hike through the mountains and had given it to her there and then.

He hadn't for one moment imagined she

would have kept it. It had been a throwaway gift with real sentiment. Yet there it was, mounted in her mother's bracelet as if it was the most important thing in the world. He had wondered why she wouldn't relinquish it to the mugger. Now he knew. She refused to forget him, refused to let go, and after his entire life had been erased, that bracelet had been her last connection to him.

He guided her through the adjoining door, pulling it closed behind him. His lips found hers again as he scooped her into his arms, carrying her up the stairs, back to the bed where her scent still lingered. But he had more things in mind than letting her rest. She remembered him, her body remembered him. She grabbed the collar of his shirt, pulling it desperately over his head as his lips sought to claim each and every part of her exposed flesh in desperate kisses to show her just how much he'd missed her.

There were no more questions, no more obstacles between them but for their clothing, something he intended to remedy. He lost himself to her taste, the soft mewling sounds she had only ever made for him. Her short nails sunk into his back in sweet torture as she pulled him closer, giving herself freely and desperately through tears that tasted of joy and sadness as he kissed them away.

Right now, in this moment, there was just the two of them, but he knew in his heart they had never been two, their souls had always been one. They belonged to one another. He was hers and she was his. It would make the pain he would bring her so much harder, which was all the more reason to counterbalance the scales now.

CHAPTER 10

Maya lay still, breathing slowly, savouring his scent and his taste upon her lips. For just the briefest moment she thought her mind had played the cruelest trick. Her fingers twitched, relishing in the invisible sparks as she traced the contours she had once known by heart. He had changed a little in the last three years.

Hard work had further sculpted his muscles, and he had new scars, some she could identify, others she could only guess as to what had caused them. She enjoyed discovering his every minor alteration, drinking him in as she explored his body in the same thorough manner he studied hers.

A content sigh slipped unguarded through her lips as her eyes opened. Her head tilted from its position on his chest to look at the sleeping man tangled in her embrace. It was really him, he was really here. They lay intertwined, pressed tightly against each other in the single bed. She allowed herself a moment to watch him, to listen to his heart, his breathing, to relish what they had shared.

She had felt so many overpowering emotions when she realised it really was him in the café. In that moment, she had forgotten to be angry, she had forgotten the hurt and pain, and had been swallowed by the relief at finding him alive, unhurt. Need had taken over; she had pressed his lips, trying to force him to look at her, to see if he still remembered her.

For a moment, as he had failed to respond, she feared she had been forgotten. When he finally returned her kiss, the only feeling that consumed her had been of his lips on hers, their bodies against one another as he stoked her internal fires and made her burn. She rode the tide of elation, of the joy of their reunion. All other thoughts had been forgotten.

Until now.

That moment had passed. Even as she lay there basking in his glory, savouring the sensation of his arm wrapped around her possessively, she could feel the anger in her core beginning to boil.

He had left her without a word. For three years, she didn't know if he was alive, dead, or even real.

The questions she managed to force through her lips had been silenced with kisses, her pain soothed by the pleasure of his touch. Now she felt like a fool. He had left her without so much as a word, and instead of seeking answers, she surrendered to her body's desires. All the time she looked for him, grieved for him, he had been living here, in the same city. Who did that, and how had he made everyone forget he had ever existed?

The more she watched him sleep, the more her relief was overcome with anger. She slipped from his arms. A slight groan from his lips caused her stomach to clench, the woeful sound playing with her heart, telling her even in slumber the loss of their contact distressed him.

Right now she needed to think, and it was not something she could do so close to his intoxicating presence. Pulling her clothes on, she slipped out, using the hidden adjoining door into the café, thankful it had been left ajar.

Lewis stiffened as she entered, throwing a

towel over his shoulder before offering her a knowing wink, causing a blush to spread across her cheeks. He had seen their reunion, heard how her body responded. She only hoped the ceiling was thick and his knowledge of their deeds ended when the door to the bedsit closed.

"What can I get you?"

"Coffee, please," she whispered, fishing out her purse. He waved it away before grabbing the jug of percolator coffee. It was the afternoon. There were a few occupied tables, families who had collected their children from school and were now enjoying an evening meal or snack together.

"So how do you know Ray?" Lewis questioned, turning back to her, placing the mug on the spotless counter. Her glare must have spoken volumes because he tugged slightly on his apron, pulling it down before he met her eyes. "So, you remembered him?"

"Remembered him?" she choked, feeling the angry tears burning in her eyes. "Remembered him!" She couldn't find the words.

She couldn't find a way to verbalise that for three years she had done everything she could think of to find him, that she had given up her career to gain access to a better database, used her job to search the streets. That for years she had listened to her colleagues whisper about make-believe boyfriends and psychotic breaks following her father's death, about how she almost lost herself to grief, not only because her father had died, but because the person she loved, the one person she needed to lean on for support had vanished, leaving her alone, taking the two most important people in her life away and the breath from her lungs in one fell swoop. How there hadn't been a day of her life where she didn't think about him, where she hadn't searched for him in the faces of strangers, when her heart hadn't felt as if it had been shattered into a million pieces that could never be reunited because the most vital piece, him, was missing, and without him, she had known she could never be whole again.

It wasn't until she inhaled she realised she *had* found the words, that every thought had come pouring from her. Worse still, as she averted her gaze from a shocked looking Lewis, she saw Raiden standing in the doorway, a stricken look upon his face, his hand grasping the doorjamb as if it was the only thing keeping him upright.

~

He had felt the loss of her warmth even through the best night's sleep he'd had in years. Summer sun had turned to Arctic wind, and his skin mourned her loss. He was used to the cold, but this was a different chill, internal, intrinsic, unbearable. Pulling on his hoodie, he made a half-dash towards the door, thrusting one foot then the other into his jeans as he hopped along frantically, fearing she was about to leave.

Relief enveloped him as he saw her at the café's counter, accepting a coffee from his cousin. They were talking quietly, but it had been impossible to miss a single heartbreaking word that streamed from her mouth. He never realised how much suffering his actions had caused.

For him, she had given up the thing she loved most up in the world. All this time he thought her sparkle had faded because her father had died, that she had left surgery because it held too many memories of him. But it hadn't been her father to blame. It had been him. Just as it was his fault that someone now hunted for her. Had she stayed in surgery, she would never have known her gift. No one would have realised what she was. Damn it. He'd left to protect her, but his actions had done just the opposite.

Raiden watched a flush of embarrassment spread across her cheeks. She turned to leave, the steaming mug abandoned on the counter, her mind at war with her heart. Her vision fixed on the door as its bell rang, causing her eyes to briefly connect with the person who had just entered and was holding the door for the family who were leaving.

"I'm glad you're safe, Raiden," she whispered without looking back as her shoulders slumped. He could almost hear the pained sigh that escaped her lips.

As he stared at her, wondering if she would stay or go, he saw the figure saunter inside. His long hair was secured back into a ponytail, making his oblong face seem somehow more severe. His intense brown eyes flicked from him to Maya, where they remained, and Raiden knew full well it was more than the curve of her hips that had him fixated. He knew this man, Zaz, the Thorne family appraiser, and his piercing gaze captured Maya like a deer in the headlights.

Shit. She didn't even realise the danger. Raiden's world moved in slow motion as she lifted her head to look at the approaching figure. If he touched her, it was game over. He may have already seen too much.

In six long strides, Raiden grabbed Maya's elbow, bustling her through the door and down the street, his pace almost a run. He was aware of her difficulty keeping up, of her quiet protests, but only when he was certain they weren't being followed did he stop.

"We need to talk." Maya opened her mouth, and the fire in her eyes warned him she was about to object. "It's important."

"I have to get ready for work. Come home after."

Home, the thought almost teased a smile from his lips. Despite everything she still thought of her house as their home. She reached into her bag, producing an envelope containing a spare key, an act that brought a smile to his lips. Even though she hadn't found him at the time, the envelope bore his name. "I had the locks changed."

"You're not on rota." He wasn't sure why he challenged her, he just knew that he didn't want her to walk away from him. Even with a key in his hand, he couldn't bear to watch her leave.

"I'm covering. I get off at eight." She moved to leave, but he was quicker moving his arms, boxing her in against the wall. He was so close he could feel her breath on his neck as he prevented her retreat.

"Are we okay?"

"I don't know what we are. I am unbelievably

angry at you right now." He knew the only reason she whispered was because she still hadn't learnt to express her anger as anything more than tears. "But, more the fool me, I still love you. I never stopped. I'll listen to everything you have to say, but I won't promise you more than that. I won't be hurt by you again."

"I can accept those terms," he whispered, lowering his head to kiss her forehead. "I never meant to hurt you. You were meant to forget me."

"If you thought I could ever forget you, you really don't know me as well as you thought you did. My place, eight-thirty. Bring breakfast."

"Until then, and Maya." He leaned forwards, his lips zeroing in on the sensitive spot on her neck he knew would turn her to putty in his hands, but she moved too quickly, her fingers pressing on his lips, pushing him away gently.

"No, you don't get to kiss this away."

"That's not what you were saying earlier," he growled seductively as she ducked from under his arm.

"Extenuating circumstances."

"Oh?" he flashed a seductive smile.

"Yes, I was horny, you were available. You're just lucky I saw you before I got to Lewis."

He could tell she regretted the words the moment they left her lips, even if he knew they were meant in jest. She bit back an apology as she turned to leave. Damn it, he couldn't let her walk away. His hand was on her shoulder, spinning her as he pulled her to his chest, his lips crashing against hers with a fierce claim.

"You're mine, Maya. Perhaps I need to remind your body who owns it." He heard her moan as he began trailing kisses down her neck, her futile resistance more encouraging than geared towards pushing him away.

"Who are you again?" she breathed huskily, digging her fingers into his back as her knees weakened. She squealed as he lifted her into his arms.

"Maybe I need to remind you again. When I am through with you, the only name you'll know will be mine." He heard her swallow. She didn't need to be at work for a few hours yet, despite what she had implied, and he had no intention of letting her go. The last place Zaz would look for her was right above the shop they just left. He couldn't be certain he'd seen her for what she was, but one way or another, being seen together was damning.

∾

With a still flushed and breathless Maya safely seen to work, Raiden knew he could no longer delay the inevitable. Entering the café, he noticed it was strangely empty. As his eyes panned the booths and tables, he noticed there was only one occupied, the one at the rear of the café. The way Lewis caught his gaze, inclining his head, told him everything he needed to know about the sole patron.

"Blaze." Zaz extended his hand across the table, acknowledging his old friend. "That's a hot piece of ass I saw you with earlier. She got a name?" the black-haired figure questioned as Raiden dropped into the seat opposite him. Zaz looked to his unaccepted hand and chuckled, pulling it back.

"Maya, with a capital mmm." Raiden grinned. Small truths. Zaz would have discovered her name the moment Raiden had taken her from the café in a manner that had been anything but subtle. The only thing working for him was that Zaz knew him well enough to know he kept business and personal life separate. "So what you been up to? It's been what, a year now?" He and Zaz had risen the ranks together, both taken in by the family. At one point they had been as thick as thieves, had each other's backs more times than he could count. But their friendship of old wouldn't stop Zaz doing his job.

Business before Buddies, every time. Which was why when Raiden ensured the Thorne family had no recollection of Maya, the numbers of people whose memories he targeted and short-circuited were very few. The Thorne family played everything close to their chest, so the chances of compromise were minimal. Only three people knew of Maya's existence as leverage for her father, and after his death, their knowledge of her vanished just as Raiden had in the eyes of everyone else.

"There about. I'll forgive you for keeping me waiting. If I was tapping that, I'd be late too. I trust I was expected?"

"Nothing finalised, didn't realise you were stopping by for me. I knew you'd be coming, though. I was told you'd keep away from my workplace. This boss gets a little touchy when my other boss scares off his patrons." Raiden tried to shrug noncommittally, forcing himself to relax. The last thing he needed was for Zaz to learn something important from him.

"Fair enough, fair enough. I was told to send you an invitation, but since I was here anyway, I thought I'd wait for you to come back." Zaz lifted his shoulders this time. "I'm here to exchange notes."

"Down to business then. I've isolated the reaper to the medical profession, specifically the medics. That hot piece of ass, as you call her, is my way in. I now know they comply to a four-on-four-off shift rota, but the things we are seeing are sporadic."

"Are they?" He quirked an eyebrow. Raiden's mind cursed, he couldn't tell if Zaz was playing with him or genuinely asking.

"There's no one shift that has covered each of the seven subjects at the point they were revived, and since shift covers aren't updated on the rota service I have access to, I'm checking who covers shifts with my piece of ass." Please buy it. Raiden offered a silent prayer. This conversation was make-or-break. He needed to get Maya off the radar.

"You know, I've seen her face before." Zaz tapped his chin thoughtfully before clicking his fingers, a staged gesture. Since neither of them had ever been able to get a good read on the other, the fact he'd made this obviously fake response caused Raiden's skin to prickle. Zaz definitely knew something. "Wasn't she the one who did the surgery of the financial director? He was on your hit list too, wasn't he?"

He knows, was all that went through Raiden's mind at that moment. He tried to keep his expression neutral, his pulse from racing.

"I checked out her and her partner, I don't see any evidence of—"

"You don't think the fact she transferred to the medics just before we saw this occur is a correlation?"

This time he felt the ground beneath him warp. As far as anyone else was concerned, he'd only been on the trail a matter of weeks. Yes, he'd been investigating on his own for the last six months, but not within Thorne's sights. He wracked his brain, appearing to give his words due consideration.

"Correlation does not equal causation. Although you're right, she was the last one hired, but that was two years ago, so why the need for pyres now, why not then? This inconsistency is another reason I am cosying up to her. That and she's a damn good lay. Sex loosens lips and dulls inhibition." Good, that was good. All truth. He just wished Zaz wasn't so difficult to read. Had they discovered his other smouldering ashes? He'd been so careful, and the Blue Coats mentioned nothing of his other murders in the news.

"So you're going to fuck a confession from

her?" Raiden tried to grin as Zaz watched him over the brim of the almost empty teacup. "You've got one week, Blaze, and then I take what I know to the boss. You know how he likes Luiza to handle interrogations."

"A week?" He felt the frown pull on his brow. It was clear Zaz already knew enough to take theories to the boss. He'd been brought in to do just that. So, why was he showing leniency, was it because he had an in with the medics, or had he noticed something else?

"Yes, a week, because in all the years you've worked for us, she's the first woman you've brought home, and the only person I've ever heard call you by your first name."

Raiden felt his mask begin to crack. Fuck. Weakness exposed.

CHAPTER 11

$\mathcal{M}$aya gave an exhausted sigh, pulling her car into the driveway before killing the engine. The neighbours had been busy this morning. The scent of freshly mowed grass carried with it the fresh scent of bacon on the cool morning breeze.

At this time of morning, the neighbourhood bristled with life. The quiet tones of chatter as parents began hurrying their children on the way to school were punctuated with the sounds of engines roaring to life while partners kissed each other goodbye before they left for work.

She took a moment just to stand by her car, to appreciate a landscape that seemed more vibrant than just yesterday. Autumn's lips had kissed the trees, causing their once green flesh to erupt in a beautiful blush of crimsons and oranges while the wind's fingers teased them, causing them to wilt at the mastery of its touch.

She found herself blushing as she set the alarm on her device for an hour earlier than normal. The butterflies in her stomach became excited at the thought of Raiden finally coming home to her. When he crossed her threshold, she wanted to look her best, to remind him exactly what he had left behind.

Opening the door, she kicked off her shoes, realising the delicious aroma that had been teasing her had not been from another house, but from hers. With a smile she couldn't stop spreading, she placed her shoes on the rack where they belonged, next to his.

Following her nose, she stopped as she saw the sliding partition between the lounge and the dining room had been left open, revealing a beautifully set table. Her books and papers had been tidied away to their places on the bookshelf, and the tablecloth she had left folded in one of the drawers adorned the candlelit table. The candles flickered on the polished candelabrum that for years had been left to gather dust on the fireplace. She raised a hand to her chest, lost for words.

"It'll be ready in just a moment, there's tea in the pot, decaf. I know you need to sleep." Closing her eyes, Maya let the sound of his voice wash over her for but a moment before pulling herself back to her senses.

"Raiden, what are you doing here?" she whispered softly. He emerged from the kitchen, with a spatula in hand and a grin on his face. His fingers folded around her hand, capturing it completely as he led her to the table, pulling out a chair as he waited for her to sit.

"You said half-eight." His hands rubbed her shoulders gently, teasing a slight moan from her lips as she allowed herself to relax. She'd forgotten how wonderful this room looked bathed in candlelight. The curtains had been drawn, shutting out the morning's first light so the soft glow reflected on the varnished surfaces, creating small bulbs of light in the polished wood of the panelled walls. Beads from the crystal chandelier above sparkled like starlight casting rainbows down upon the linen tablecloth.

"I meant this evening." Something about the way he smiled told her he had known exactly when she had meant.

"You said bring breakfast."

"But it's tea time."

"So I made an English breakfast, straight

from those Victorian novels you used to read." He glanced to the bookshelves as if to suggest he noticed there weren't any there any more, an action that caused her to wonder how long he had been home if he had already picked up on such minor details.

"Most of them are in Dad's—I mean, my study after Rick tried to throw them out. He had this ridiculous notion that no woman of his should read romance. Probably didn't want them to realise what they were missing. The only reason he left the textbooks is he thought they were too complex for little old me." The displeased furrowing of his brow did little to ruin the sight of him pouring her a cup of tea before returning to the kitchen in time for her to hear the toaster pop. She looked towards the ceiling, blinking quickly to dispel the slight blurring of her eyes before the threatening tears could be seen. Gods she'd missed him.

"How was your day?" he kissed the crown of her head, placing the plate before her. Moments later, they enjoyed a hot meal, and she told him about her day, her week, her life since he had left, and he asked questions, listening with a breathtaking smile that told her all she needed to know, that he had missed this as much as she had.

It felt so good to share a table with him again, to talk to him, that she had almost forgotten she was meant to be angry. She gave a slight shrug, deciding then and there not to try to hold on to her anger and simply enjoy this second chance. "Come on then, beautiful, time to get off to bed. Do you want me to come back later?"

"Are you still a night owl?" A few weeks after they had first got together, Raiden had changed his life for her, completing his work at night, mirroring her hours as closely as possible. They never seemed to have enough time together, and he had done everything he could to squeeze those extra minutes together, even if it was just sleeping together in the same bed as the sun tracked across the sky.

"Always."

"Then stay, we will talk in the morning."

"The evening," he corrected with a chuckle. She grabbed his hand, leading him upstairs, hesitating outside the bedroom door. Their bedroom door, not the one she had shared with Rick.

"Raiden," she watched his face grow serious at her tone, "if you're not here when I wake up, I'll never forgive you."

"I'll be here."

Glancing down at her feet, Maya felt her cheeks burn at the state of her hiking boots. Their once supple leather had dulled and cracked from years of neglect. She and Raiden had always gone hiking in the mountains, but after his disappearance, aside from those first few weeks where she had walked every trail until her feet were raw with blisters, she had thrust them to the back of her wardrobe and locked them away for good. She had to admit she missed coming here, missed seeing the beautiful flowers in bloom and the feeling of serenity.

Looking down across the valley was breathtaking, sprays of reds, oranges and yellows from the trees below battled for dominance against the striking colours of the setting sun, both erupting in such colour it was impossible not to stand and stare with bated breath. They stood hand in hand until the sun dipped below the horizon, basking in the glow as much as the experience of sharing something so magnificent.

"I'm not sure why you wanted to bring me out here to talk," Maya said, breathing in the crisp autumn air as they continued along the trail. They were running late. The plan had been to sit and watch the sunset from their special place, but the view from where they had stood had been just as captivating. How could it be she had forgotten how to appreciate the simple beauty of the world around her without him in her life?

"Out here, no one will hear you scream." Her breath hitched at his innuendo, and she shook her head, dispelling the thought of his naked body, his hair of storms and starlight backdropped against the clear night sky. "Come on, don't tell me you can't keep up?" he teased as she froze in place at the thought.

"I'm not the one bringing up the rear," she quipped, glancing over her shoulder.

"I just happen to prefer the view back here." He slapped her backside playfully before wrapping his arms around her. Turning into his embrace, she watched as the smile reflected in his eyes dulled slightly. The minty scent of his slow exhale, and the way he dropped his gaze towards the soft grass at their feet, told her he was ready to talk. "Now, let's set up the blanket. I have a lot to tell you. I can't tell you everything, but I'll tell you what I can. The rest will have to wait."

And he did. Maya had known before he disappeared the things he had turned his hand to. He had been sworn into the service of the

Thorne family when he was nineteen, three years before they met. Apparently they hadn't realised that the Blaze family had any remaining heirs and had been about to write off the debt when he ended up being detained with one of their new members for assault with a deadly weapon. That day sealed his fate. He was given two choices, he could pay the debt, which was an exorbitant fee, or he could work it off by doing jobs for their family.

He had been working for them for nine years now, but three years ago, things had gotten dangerous. The Thorne family started a power-play to overthrow Vincent Masters, the vampire leader of Overton's underground networks. He knew even before the first blood had been split that they had bitten off more than they could chew. Master's connections had run far higher and deeper than his boss had realised.

Three years ago, the silent war erupted, families were slaughtered, the loved ones of anyone serving the Thorne family turning up dead. That was when he had disappeared. It followed shortly after the death of Maya's father. He had hated the thought of leaving her at such a time, but it was the only way to keep her safe, both from the war and the family he served. Using his lightning alignment, he short-circuited the neural networks of everyone who had ever seen his face, anyone who knew about the two of them, erasing himself from their lives for their protection.

"I left you for last," he sighed, bringing his story to a close. "I didn't realise it hadn't worked. It had been successful for everyone except Lewis, but that's because we share blood."

"So all this time, you thought you were keeping me safe?" Her heart began to ache. She had imagined so many reasons why he may have left that day, but her safety had never been a consideration.

"There's more, Maya, more I need to tell you." It was impossible to miss the sadness in his words.

"I think that's enough for tonight," she whispered, moving to straddle him. She placed her hand upon his chest, pushing him back onto their blanket. Being here with him now was enough. She didn't need any more answers than he'd already given. "Of course it wouldn't work on me. Don't you know true love nullifies all curses."

"Are you saying you love me?" His low voice rumbled as she kissed his neck.

"I hear actions speak louder than words. Let

me show you my answer. Out here, no one will hear you scream."

"Damn it," his voice wavered as her hand dropped to his trousers, causing his Adam's apple to bob, "you stole my line."

"And you stole my heart," she whispered with a kiss.

Maya was surprised how quickly she slipped back into life with Raiden. She had missed sharing meals, their mornings watching movies, talking, or playing before sleeping the day away to awake before her shift. She could get used to him cooking, to the smell of something other than just the ready meals she had been living off. But at the back of her mind, she still felt that bud of insecurity. Every evening when she awoke, she expected to find him gone, vanished from her life again without a trace.

The more she allowed herself to enjoy it, the more this doubt blossomed. She tossed and turned, haunted by nightmares, right until her watch vibrated on her wrist. Half-six. It was far later than she intended to sleep, but Raiden was still beside her, his arm wrapped tightly around her while his breath teased her shoulder with its soft caress.

With last night's dream so prominent in her mind, she slipped from his embrace. There was only one way to ensure she would always find him. She couldn't face another three years of not knowing, or worse, him succeeding in stripping her memories and removing the best part of her life. He had no right to do that to her, and despite what she had said that night on the mountains, she could not be certain that he wouldn't succeed should he feel the need to try again. There was only one solution. One way to ensure no matter what happened she would always know how to find him.

Tiptoeing downstairs, she found where he left his device charging. She knew she was being insecure, irrational, but it didn't matter. Using his pin—her birthday—she installed the Tracking-Mate app on his device, pairing it with her own. If he ever planned to disappear again, she would find him and drag him back. She wasn't going through this again.

As the pairing finished, she placed it on hidden mode. A feature designed to ensure no one knew you had the app, let alone were paired to someone. Doing this meant only the paired partner could disable the link, which prevented any tampering. Only she could turn it off. Until then, she would always know where he was, always be able to find him. As the app faded from his screen, she noticed something else.

She knew she should have known better, that given the people he worked for even looking at the document could be a death sentence, and yet the way it popped up as the app closed made it impossible to ignore. Her fingers danced across the screen before her mind even finished warning her it was wrong.

Maya's hands rarely shook, but the device began to tremble in her grasp as she looked at the contents, at the list of names—crossed out names —all of which were familiar. They were people whose lives she had saved. There were dates and locations. Who in their right mind put something so condemning on a spreadsheet? Who even made a spreadsheet to begin with? The last nine names were the murders attributed to Pyre-starter.

The device slipped from her grasp as Raiden appeared on the stairs. She couldn't control the way she stared, the way her lips parted in a silent scream. He must have seen the terror in her eyes, the device at her feet on the plush carpet, because his arms were around her before she had a chance to run, before she'd realised he'd moved from the stairs.

His hand pressed across her mouth, silencing the scream that bubbled up from within her as he pulled her body into his. She could hear him talking, whispering, as she tossed her head from side to side, trying to escape his grip. She pushed him away, clawed at him with limbs weighed down by fear, but he was bigger, stronger. His leg swept behind her, throwing her off balance. He lowered her to the floor. His weight straddling her, a single hand pinned her arms above her head with ease as she thrashed, trying to shake free of his crushing weight.

"Maya. Calm down." His grip was tight, bordering on painful, but she refused to stop. She needed to get away. He had killed all those people, all the people she had saved. She couldn't breathe. The pain of his betrayal, of her own foolishness, crushed her lungs with its vice-like grip.

Air froze in her throat with precious little completing the journey through the fear-constricted airways. "Maya, listen to me. It's not what it looks like." He removed his hand from her mouth to drag it down his face. She wanted to scream, but she couldn't even breathe. "Fuck," he cursed.

"It's you," she choked out, her chest heaving in panic as dark motes swarmed across her vision. Her mind was getting foggy but still racing. What was it Detective Mendel had said? That it was possible the killer had fixated on her, that she was his end goal. He'd come back to her to finish what he started and, even knowing what he did for a living, like a fool she'd let him in.

But the detective also said it could be nothing. She'd wanted to believe that.

She looked for her belt. If they could see this they'd know she was in danger, send someone to help her, but she was still in her nightgown. The camera was useless shut away in her wardrobe, hidden away so if anyone viewed the footage they wouldn't witness her most intimate moments. She was trapped. Raiden was Pyre-starter, and she was trapped in her home with him.

"Breathe, Maya, breathe or you're going to—"

"You killed them!" she squealed, not recognising her own voice through the thick terror lining it.

"Sweetheart, breathe." He traced his hand down her face, cupping her cheek, trying to make her look at him, trying to calm her as she thrust her head back and forth away from his touch. She hated he could restrain her so effortlessly with a single hand, that no matter what she did she couldn't escape him, even more than that, she hated the part of her buried somewhere beneath the panic and fear that still responded to his touch. "I didn't kill them."

"I saw your list," she wheezed, tears squeezed from her eyes.

"I didn't kill them. They were already dead. Now breathe, sweetheart, come on, deep breaths. If you pass out, I won't have chance to explain." She saw the fear in his eyes, the weight of worry, the vulnerability. It wasn't fair. Murderers shouldn't have eyes like these, eyes so filled with heartbreak.

"Are you going to kill me?" She choked back a sob and saw the pain on his face as his grip slackened slightly.

"Maya, sweetheart, I've been protecting you. Don't you see? The people on that list, they were meant to be dead. Stay dead."

"Hits?"

"No, honey. You brought them back, but... not really. I had to take care of them. I thought I could keep your secret hidden, but just over a month ago, the Thorne family discovered the existence of a reaper.

"It was my fault, I was seen disposing of a body. I didn't want them tracking it back to you,

so I told them it was the first, that's when I
started setting the pyres. Part of me thought if I
made a display of it that, with the media
coverage, you'd realise what the victims had in
common. When that didn't work, I sent you the
pictures. If I could make you stop, the trail they
wanted me to follow would go cold, and you'd
stay safe." His face was so close to hers now she
could feel his cool breath chilling the trails of her
tears.

"Reaper?"

"A Perennial, perhaps necromancer is the
easiest way to explain it for the moment. The
people on my list, they weren't alive, not really.
You brought them back by tethering part of their
soul to the corpse.

"I wasn't sure why they were getting on
with their lives as if nothing happened, not
until I saw what you were doing. You
commanded their bodies to work, you told them
they would be getting back to their life in no
time. They were obeying you because that's
what reapers do, control the essence of the
dead.

"Normally a reaper feeds on the energy of a
being under their command, but you were
discharging them from service, letting them get
on with their life as if nothing had happened,

which, I think, is why you always felt so fatigued afterwards."

"Your lying," she sobbed. That couldn't be true. She'd seen the films, necromancers were evil, drawn to the darkness, to domination, to raising the dead and making them further their evil ambitions. That wasn't her, that wasn't who she was. She protected life, not commanded the dead. He had to be wrong, but his tone, his body language, the look in his eyes, everything about him told her it was true. Gods, she was evil. She robbed the dead of their peace.

"Maya, I wish I was. I found the first one about six months ago. An old man, he'd fallen down a cliff, his bones were shattered, his skin decomposing. I freed him the only way I knew how, by incinerating the body to burn away the tether. I started to get this weird sensation around others. The more I found, the more I saw the pattern. I had found four when I realised why the charge I was feeling felt so familiar. I'd only ever felt like that once before, when you touched me.

"I started to follow you, sure enough, I saw you do it. I saw the energy of their souls leave and you bind part of them to the corpse. Just a few weeks ago, after the first public pyre, the

Thorne family discovered another when one of their hits came back from the dead.

"He'd been dosed with enough poison to fell an elephant, but the next day he was walking around like nothing had happened. That's when they sent me to investigate further. After all, as far as they knew I had already found one. They wanted me to discover who was responsible. The problem was, I already knew. That man who was eyeing you in the café, his name was Zaz. He was there to take over because I was moving too slowly. I don't think he bought it when I said you were someone I was just sleeping with."

"This is too much, Raiden," she whispered. "Let go of me."

"Maya."

"Raiden Blaze, let go of me," she snapped. She pushed up on her arms weakly, relieved when he released his grip.

"Don't run from me, Maya," he warned, standing, releasing her fully from beneath him. She pushed herself away until her back touched the wall, her gaze fixed upon him. He stood looking at her as if he bore the weight of the world on his shoulders and it was crashing down around him. How dare he look at her like that after what he had just told her? "Talk to me."

"Leave."

"Maya." He crouched before her, retracting his hand as she flinched away from his touch.

"It's too much. I need to think." She saw him nod as he fished her key from his pocket, extending it towards her. She felt her fingers twitch, her mind telling her to take it from him, to protect herself. "Keep it. I just... I need some space right now."

"As you wish." His hand rested on the door. When he looked back towards her, she could see his world dissolving in the welling shimmer of his gaze. "I love you, Maya," she heard him whisper as the door closed behind him. Maya lost herself to tears, hugging her knees as she sat against the wall.

She wasn't sure how long she sat there, but eventually her body began to function again. Dragging herself to the shower, she walked in a daze, getting ready for work. She threaded her belt through her jeans, and before she knew it, she was parked outside the ambulance station, her eyes still red from the tears. Raiden Blaze had broken her heart, again, and this time she was to blame.

CHAPTER 12

*R*aiden stood outside of Maya's door for several moments, his forehead pressed to the barrier between them that was so much larger than the red wooden door that separated them. He had intended to tell her everything that night in the mountains, but she had swept him away, removed his ability to think.

He wanted to say that his reaction to her was the only reason he had delayed the truth, but he knew better. There had been other opportunities, but he hadn't been able to broach the subject. He knew that telling her what he had done, what she had done, would break her heart.

He couldn't bring himself to go straight

home, so he lingered in the neighbourhood, waiting to catch a glimpse of her so he could gauge how she was feeling, see if she was okay. Okay? He knew she would be anything but; however, she carried her burdens well. He remained close, used to hiding in the shadows and disappearing in plain sight, until he saw her car pull away. Her eyes were rimmed red, her shoulders only slightly slumped. She looked better than he expected.

In no hurry to sit up all night and brood, he decided to take a slow stroll home. It was a lovely area. The twilight glow of the evening sky captured the park in its coming transition, the metamorphosis as day changed to night. It had been constructed for beauty both in darkness and light, as the night came the day-blooming flowers bowed their heads in sleep, making way for the night bloomers that would drink in the moonlight and thrive in the soft glow of the lampposts.

He listened to the birds singing their evening chorus as he moved to sit on one of the many benches overlooking the vast greenery. A few children played ball with their overenthusiastic pet, their carefree laughter drifting on a wind that held winter's first kiss. He watched the large dog tear across the grass, leaping in feats of seemingly impossible acrobatics to seize the yellow ball within its drooling mouth.

Maya being on shift tonight was a blessing. Work focused her mind, and he knew, no matter what, she'd be safe. After a night of distraction, he would try to talk to her again. She had asked him to stay away not realising she asked the impossible.

He had managed to keep his distance for so long, but their separation was not something he could endure again. It had all but destroyed him the first time, even though he threw himself into his work, becoming only Blaze as he tried to forget he was ever Raiden, that his life had once had balance. He had almost convinced himself that, after she had processed the information he had dumped on her, she would be able to forgive him when his device chimed. Seeing the emergency code word from his cousin, his fingers connected the call immediately.

"Ray, thank goodness." There was an edge to Lewis' voice he didn't like. "They were here, Ray, asking questions about your girlfriend. I think they know. When I didn't have any information for them, they wanted to know if I had any idea where they could find you. Apparently, something is interfering with the tracking data. They spun a line about you being seen staggering away from an accident and asked if you'd go to your girlfriend's. I told them I had no idea, that I'd only seen her twice."

"Did they hurt you?" he growled. The anger in his voice saw a young couple swerve aside, giving him a wide berth as he marched to only his feet knew where. His bike, no, a car. He needed a car. A rental.

"No, just questions, Ray. I'm just your landlord and employer after all." It was a ruse they had kept up since Lewis first offered him the flat above his cafe. The family had asked why he needed to work, and he had spun them a line about Lewis' poor record-keeping coming in handy if he ever needed to provide an alibi.

"They seemed more interested in finding Maya than you, though." Raiden glanced to his device. He knew Maya's neighbourhood was a dead zone for device tracking which—since all family members had their chips removed on induction—would have been the only way to pinpoint him.

The Thorne family had ensured that this entire block was blacked out when they strong-armed Maya's father into being their emergency off-the-books surgeon by using his young daughter's safety as leverage. Black areas meant that there was a family-friendly in the area, and no matter what, it was an unspoken rule the healers remained unharmed because ultimately they would help anyone, regardless of their alignment.

When he met Maya six years ago, there had been nothing accidental about it. The only accident was the instant attraction he had felt. The Thorne family had wanted a surgeon, the best. But her father had been getting cold feet. Knowing what he did, Raiden was never sure if it was because he was worried about his illness, or them discovering Maya followed in his footsteps. Raiden had sworn to her old man he would keep her protected, off their radar when she qualified because, despite his reasons for coming into their life, he loved her.

Raiden knew very little about what happened before they had sent him to keep a watch on the family, only that he had been their surgeon for over a decade to keep his baby girl safe. When his hands began to tremble, Raiden's presence was required to make sure he was on hand in case illness made the man's lips loose.

He had been an excellent surgeon and had saved many lives during his time with them. His service earned him the opportunity to live his remaining days in peace for so long as his lips remained sealed. When he had died three years ago Raiden had erased Maya from their minds and, to protect her from the silent war, he had erased himself from everyone but the Thorne family's mind, destroying any evidence he had ever lived, except for the memories he stored in his own secret place, the photos and videos of their time together.

"You think they know?"

"Worse. I think they know *you* know. Zaz looked pissed."

"Thanks for the heads-up." He cursed under his breath. She would be safe at work, there was too much visibility, but the moment she left the safety of the station, she would be unprotected, fair game. The only advantage he had at this moment was that she was shift covering, her name wasn't on the rota. If they were looking for her, waiting for her, they would wait at her home. Picking up the rental, he parked a few spaces away from her car, counting down until her shift finished.

His eyes had been closed, but the moment she stepped from the building, he felt the charge of her upon his skin. Stepping from the car as she walked past, he hooked his hand on her elbow, guiding her quickly towards the passenger door.

"Raiden, I—"

"Leave with me now." During their three

years together, these words became more than just those spoken on the dance floor. He had whispered them countless times. She came to understand that whenever these words left his lips, they needed to go, although he had never told her why. Each time he saw a familiar face, each time he felt the prickle of danger or wanted to steal her away, these four words had kept her safe. He prayed they were engraved into her heart as much as any *I love you* he had spoken.

"But—"

"Not a debate. Get in the car." He saw her glance over her shoulder before sighing and sliding into the passenger's side. The way she crossed her arms and pulled her lips into a pout made him chuckle, but he knew he was in trouble. Sliding into the driver's side, he locked the doors before bringing the engine quietly to life.

"What part of I need time—"

"Maya, I want nothing more than to give you the time you need. But right now I can't. Safety trumps reverence. I need you safe."

"Safe?"

"Despite my best efforts, the Thorne family discovered who you are. I'm taking you to my safe house. I need you to lie low for a few days until I find out who knows what and, you know," he tapped his forehead, "resolve what I can. The thing is, like with my debt, there may be too much of a trail to secure you completely. Until I find out what I'm dealing with, I need you to sit tight. You'll have plenty of time to think there. I'll respect your wishes, but please, do this for me, let me keep you safe." He felt his shoulders relax as Maya nodded her consent.

The safe house was only a five-minute drive from town. It was a small property on a busy road standing almost adjacent to the school. They were small houses, tightly packed together with almost non-existent front yards. Maya watched the pedestrians, the bustle of parents walking their children down the street towards the large gates. For a safe house, the street was busier than she expected. She expected him to drive out to the mountains, cutting her off from all civilisation.

"It's better to have witnesses," Raiden mumbled as if reading her thoughts. He gave her the key, making no effort to unfasten his seatbelt. "There's limited food, mainly non-perishables, but some necessities will be delivered every day. I can't promise the state of the inside. I wasn't expecting to have to use it for some time. If you need anything, message Lewis. I've put his number in your device under deli takeaway, he'll arrange whatever you need. Just... keep out of sight and wait for word."

"You're not coming in?"

"I'm trying to respect your boundaries."

She bit her lip, barely stopping herself from inviting him inside, and instead gave the slightest nod. She needed time to think, and his distraction would be all too welcome.

Sliding from the car, she took the few short strides to the front door that was separated from the pavement only by a small boundary wall and a front yard consisting solely of a foot's length of flagstones. The lack of weeds showed the property to have been maintained. In her haste to reach the door her foot caught the milk bottle holder, tipping it over. She cringed, expecting the empty glass bottle nestled inside to shatter. She gathered it up quickly, almost knocking her head on the wall-mounted mailbox, before pushing her key into the lock.

The wooden door creaked and groaned as she pushed it open. Closing it with a soft thud, she slid the chain and deadlock into place. The house had a two-up-two-down layout. The galley kitchen had been remodelled, extended to absorb what must have once been the downstairs bathroom to create a larger room with a breakfast bar. To compensate for this extra space one of the bedrooms had been divided by a thin partition wall to create a small toilet and shower room, with a room that housed the single bed and small chest of drawers.

The inside had not been maintained like the outside. A thick layer of dust coated all the surfaces, but at least someone had possessed the foresight to use dust covers on the furniture. Venting the back windows, she carefully removed the dust covers, placing them in the washing machine after confirming the backyard had a washing line. It wasn't much, a large, paved area that ran adjacent to the kitchen before ending in a large square, but the tall walls afforded her privacy, and the recoiling washing line seemed in working order.

Grabbing the sheets from the single room she added them to the machine, attempting to hold back the coughs triggered by the visible dust motes floating through the air, captured by the morning's sun as it streamed through the slightly cracked blinds. After wrestling with the water stop tap, she located a box of detergent in the under-sink cupboard and was ready to get on with the list of tasks she had assigned herself.

Tasks she knew were an excuse to avoid thinking about other things.

As long as she kept busy, she didn't need to worry about the evil nestled within her, the darkness she hadn't even known existed. Every time she closed her eyes, or when her mind was still, she saw scenes from the old movies and books where the evil necromancer stood within a sea of the dead shouting 'Arise!' as the dead broke free of their graves to do their bidding and unleash hell upon the land of the living. She needed the list. She needed to keep busy. She wasn't ready to think about this, not yet.

With the washing on, the work surfaces wiped down, and the counter-top fridge cleaned and powered up, she began to empty the cupboards and take stock of food. She dropped the saucepan and frying pan into the sink of hot water, along with the mismatched cups and plates. By the time she finished, bags of pasta, tins of tomatoes, and other tinned and packet goods lined the work surface. It would be enough to keep her fed for days, and she couldn't help but hope by the time the food was running low, she would be able to return home.

In the last cupboard, pinned down by a heavy glass paperweight, was a collection of papers, which surprised her since most things these days were sent straight to someone's device. Even letters and leaflets were a thing of the past but for rare occasions.

She shuffled through them. The first was the refuse collection days, another was the maintenance company's name and a list of their duties: window cleaning, weed removal, external repairs, the list went on. At least that explained why the outside of the building had made the house look lived-in. Amongst the numerous other invoices was a milkman itinerary. It seemed a pint of milk, and a half loaf of bread were delivered to the door every day around eight o'clock, with other items such as cheese and eggs arranged as addition once a week. It made her wonder what happened to them since clearly no one lived here, and there had been only an empty bottle outside.

Flicking through the papers, she saw everything had been arranged to give an external impression of the property being lived in, with the initial service invoices dating back over ten years.

A quick glance at her watch told her all her work had only taken two-and-a-half hours. She watched the washing machine vibrate against the tiled floor, creating an ear-piercing din as it rattled and lurched, causing the washed crockery on the draining board to rattle as it entered its final spin cycle before finally clicking off. She had known the machine was old the moment she laid eyes on it. They didn't make them like this anymore, and the wash cycles were ludicrously long.

With the sheets and dust covers on the line, she used the prop poles to hoist them higher, grateful it had been a dual line, allowing her to hang all the items she had crammed into the washer out to dry.

With that done, she ignored the rumbling in her stomach and lay on the bed. Despite her mind racing, she soon drifted into a restless slumber.

Raiden had known he was in trouble even before the cars, which had been following him since he'd circled back to check on Maya's house, had boxed him in. He had known he was in trouble from the moment Lewis had messaged him, telling him there was a car waiting outside his flat.

It had taken all of a few seconds to erase his communication data and purge his contact, and factory reset his phone. It was a single button press, to be initiated if he was ever apprehended by the Blue Coats or a rival clan.

As a fourth car screeched to a halt in front of him, he whispered a silent thank you. Things for him were bad, but at least they hadn't found him before he'd dropped Maya off. She was safe. Lewis knew what to do if he didn't hear from Raiden after their agreed time. He would look after her, get her to someone who would keep her safe. It wasn't the best option. He had wanted to avoid involving them, but they were the lesser evil, and he had promised to protect her. A promise which had no expiry date, even if his life did.

The rental car he hired possessed an anti-tracking device. The only people who knew his whereabouts would be the hire company. He didn't use a car often, only when on jobs for the boss, but someone, somewhere had spotted him. No matter the threat, the hire company couldn't track his position until his lease expired. He'd been careful, he'd rented it for a month, knowing full well he had days at most.

He relaxed his grip on the wheel, taking a long, slow breath. The emergence of ten men from the other four cars, the weapons trained upon him, told him all he needed to know. It also told him resistance was futile. If he was seen to cooperate, he could still spin a line based in truth. It all depended on exactly how much they knew. Ten men, he reminded himself. They probably knew everything.

He turned the key in the ignition, killing the engine before raising his hands as his driver's door was snatched opened by a brute of a man. A vampire. What else would he be? Most of those in the high ranks of the Thorne family were vampires. Only people such as himself and Zaz, those who had a debt to pay or extraordinary skills, were brought in from outside the species.

The vampires liked to think they owned all of Mython, and if their movements were anything to take into account, it could be true. Only the council kept things from saturation point, but they were out of touch, they had no real concept about what was happening in their country.

Unfastening his seatbelt, he stepped from the car, not giving them a chance to drag him from inside. Despite his cooperation, before he could even speak, he felt the strike. Until that point, he had always thought seeing stars had been an expression. But there they were, dancing before his vision, before darkness fell.

The first sensation he became aware of when his consciousness returned was the heavy odour of dank, decaying earth. While it was still autumn, the sun was still strong, which told him the icy chill he felt chasing across his bare chest was because of his depth rather than the cool kiss of the wind.

He knew without looking where this special corner of hell was, he had delivered many a person here before. He had even secured their limp bodies in the very shackles that now supported his weight. Shackles that blocked his energy centres and prohibited him from using his gifts.

If ever there had been any doubt, the fact he was here, like this, confirmed somehow his actions had been discovered. He was not being given a chance to defend himself. Their evidence must be damning.

He had never been present for an interrogation. Luiza liked to savour each moment of agony she inflicted alone. The Thorne family had access to many kinds of interrogator, from psychic vampires to those who preferred a more hands-on approach, and she was the worst of the worst, or the best of the best depending on which side of the wall you stood. If he was here, there was only one reason: they had discovered he had been keeping secrets from them. The question was, which ones had been exposed, Maya or—

"Avake at last." It was a female voice, rich and seductive with the slightest hint of an accent that belonged beyond the barrier. "Someone 'as been a naughty boy." He felt the sharp manicured points of her fingernails across his flesh, a warning. He doubted she was here to draw blood, although he had been wrong before. He could see her in his mind. Luiza was a dainty thing, standing at five-foot-four with kissable lips that rested in a natural pout, and eyes as cold as her heart. "I knew von day you would visit me, I 'ad 'oped it would 'ave been for something a little more... mutual. But no matter, I vill be satisfied either vay."

Finding a place on the white wall, he stared ahead. Like everything in this room, it had been designed for torture. The walls, floors, even the ceiling were white. The restraints, the chains, all white. Everything in this room was designed for sensory deprivation. The lighting had been enchanted to ensure no shadows were cast, and the air and all surfaces would remain at body temperature.

There were so many enchantments within this room to enhance its intentions that it wouldn't matter if there was any imperfection, his mind wouldn't find it. Even the chains were coated and enchanted to move in silence, his captors wore shoes designed to be silent, and should he be able to lay sight on them they would be dressed in white. The room was soundproof, not a single noise from outside would ever reach his ears.

This was Luzia's own perversion of white void torture. When his blood would stain the ground, it would vanish within a moment, absorbed so not a trace of colour remained. He had once wondered if anything in contact with the ground became white by illusion, or if the rooms simply consumed anything that did not belong.

"Do I at least get to know what I'm accused of?"

"Of course. Did you think you vould get avay with 'iding her? You knew 'ow much the boss coveted the reaper."

"The reaper?" Fuck, it *was* Maya. He had been hoping they'd uncovered his other secret.

"The girl you vere fucking."

"She's the reaper?"

"Do not play me for a fool." Raiden gritted his teeth as a cane cracked against his back, sending a burning wave of heat across his flesh that remained long after she stepped away to stand before him. She raised her chin, meeting his eyes. "Vhere did you 'ide her?"

"I don't know what you're talking about." He cried out as she struck him again, the warning of the wood as it sliced through the air did little to prepare him for the pain that followed. He sucked in a breath through bared teeth. She wasn't holding back, but if she'd drawn blood, he couldn't feel it.

"Vhere did you 'ide her?" Each word was punctuated by another agonising strike until his legs buckled beneath him, adding extra strain to his protesting shoulders as the shackles dug deeper into his wrists.

"I told you, I don't know—"

"Vrong answer." Her slender fingers grasped his chin, her nails sinking into his flesh. She forced him to look at her. "I guess ve do this the 'ard vay." Her cold lips pressed against his, the assault upon his mind instant as she devoured his energy, weakening his defences, making his mind easier to rape. *Compartmentalise,* he thought to himself, locking away his most personal thoughts, shielding them, protecting them behind barriers no force could breach. This kind of torture was its own level of hell. While not a mark was placed upon his flesh, his psyche took every raw strike.

His screams were deafening, buffered by the walls, swallowed by them despite each agonising moment echoing in his mind. He felt like his thoughts were being shredded, his mind torn apart one memory at a time as she violated his thoughts in the most painful way imaginable. This could be done with a gentle hand, but there was nothing gentle about Luiza, nothing merciful. He was too weak to fight, too exhausted to resist.

As his eyes began to flutter closed, he saw the smile upon her lips as she kept him teetering on the verge of unconsciousness. This was the place she worked best, a place where his mind was malleable.

She had stripped many secrets from spies and enemies alike in this strange betwixt. She could keep someone between life and death as easily as she could flutter her false eyelashes. She was a cruel mistress, a woman who had brought many to their knees, but she would not get what she sought from him.

He hoped.

CHAPTER 13

$\mathcal{M}$aya paced around the small house. Raiden had told her not to contact him under any circumstances, but when she'd rang the café there was something unnerving in Lewis' voice. Alarm. He'd not heard from Raiden either. With nothing but a charger and the bag she had taken to work, there was little but her racing thoughts to keep her occupied.

Her e-reader was amazing, but worry gnawed at her gut, causing her to reread the same lines, unable to focus on the amazing fantasy plot of her favourite author from beyond the barrier. Every word lost its meaning until she could bare it no longer.

She picked up her device again, her fingers

itching to send him a message, but the look on his face as she had left the car haunted her. He had been scared. He had done everything he had to keep her safe, and a single message from her could jeopardise everything he had sacrificed. She wasn't that person. No matter how much she needed to know, she wasn't going to put him at risk for her own peace of mind. But what if he was already in danger, what if his only hope lay in someone reaching out to him?

She sat. She stood. She exercised. Nothing helped. Nothing. She played with her device again, suddenly remembering she already had everything she needed, and opened the Tracking-Mate app. It seemed like months ago when she had put it on there, she had all but forgotten about it given everything else she had uncovered just seconds later. This had been designed to remain hidden, protect the user to the extent that even a complete reset didn't remove an active trace, even powered off it would utilise any source of wireless electricity to absorb enough charge to keep it active.

While devices typically required tethering to an energy port, in case of emergencies they could take energy from other sources to keep enough charge for a single SOS. If she could see his movements, at least she'd know he was safe.

The app loading screen took a painfully long time to appear. Her short nails tapped impatiently, scratching against the rough fabric of the sofa until finally the main screen appeared and her fingers glided across it to click on the active tether, aware of the tension across her forehead as her eyebrows drew into a frown she tried to remind herself to breathe. No movement for three days.

Last known location, Overton Cemetery.

Great, nothing creepy about that.

She stared at the small map, at the stationary dot showing where he was as if her gaze could somehow force it to show her his surroundings. She studied the area, following the small trail of dots that marked his route there. Then she noticed something else. She expected his device to be working on emergency power by now, but the icon on the corner of the tracker showed her it was fully charged. She wrung her hands before finally placing another call to Lewis.

"Hello, Deli take-away." His voice was etched with strain even before he knew it was her. He was as worried as she was.

"Lewis, is there any reason Raiden would visit a cemetery?" Maya pushed herself up from the sofa, walking from room to room with the device pressed to her ear, her fingers tracing nervously over every surface they could find.

"Straight to the point, no how do you do?"

"I'm serious, Lewis." She actually felt herself stamp her foot and heard the muffled impact of her socks against the tiled floor. Who did that? She glared at her foot, willing it to stay still, certain he had probably heard her mini tantrum over their connection.

"Why?"

"I put Tracking-Mate on his device in case he decided to vanish again. He's been there for three days." It was all she could do to hide the building hysteria. There was no reason to stay in such a place for so long, no reason at all. Except one. Only one thing stayed in cemeteries. Corpses. The only thing stopping her from losing her mind at this moment was the charge level of his device.

"Maybe he's lost his device." His tone didn't hint for one moment he believed the line he was spinning.

"And it still has full charge after three days, really?"

"I don't know what else to tell you, Maya." She heard Lewis thank someone as the bell chimed quietly in the background.

"Sure." Even she could hear the suspicion in

her voice. "Yeah, you're probably right," she bit. "He just left me at a safe house, promised to be back, then dropped off the face of the Earth, but not before he found some creepy ass place to tether his phone and forget it was there. It's certainly not as if he was going against the—"

"Maya, calm down."

She hadn't realised she'd rushed through every word, that she hadn't taken a single breath until his interruption.

"Raiden has been handling that family far longer than he's known you. He knows what he's doing. If he's not reaching out, it's because it would be too dangerous, to you or him. If we've still not heard from him in two days, I'll check it out myself, okay?" When she didn't answer, he prompted her again a little more firmly. "Okay?"

"Yes, fine," she snapped, throwing an empty box into the cardboard recycling with a little more force than she intended, sending the bin toppling over. She cursed, kicking the container before she began cramming the rubbish back in.

"I know it's as boring as shit there, but you've got food. Use the time to rest, okay?" The concern in his voice was unmistakable. He was worried about her, worried she was going to do something foolish, and she knew he had every reason to have such thoughts.

"I don't like this, Lewis." Her voice came out nothing more than a whisper that barely escaped through her teeth as she bit her thumbnail. Realising what she was doing, she lowered her hand.

"Me either. But he would have sent an SOS if he was in danger."

"Okay. I'll check in with you again tomorrow." Maya terminated the call, parting the curtain with her fingers. It was dark outside, the only glow on the streets came from the uniformly spaced street lamps. Looking to her device again, she gave a sigh. Lewis was probably right, but it wouldn't hurt to have her car nearby.

The streets were empty. The hospital was only a twenty-minute walk. She could park around the block, and no one would be any the wiser, and if she happened to drive past the cemetery on the way back, what harm could it do to just look?

White noise surrounded him. Not the kind of noise that was used to lull babies to sleep, but a decibel level perfectly calculated for torture. He thought silence would be his comrade here, but it seemed Luiza had other plans. The noise was deafening, never easing for a moment as it screamed its incessant hushing.

His head hurt, he could feel his grasp on everything around him slipping. He was beyond exhausted. Phantoms danced in his vision, almost hidden across the endless landscape. Every time he thought he could slip into slumber, the noise altered slightly, just enough to keep him from growing accustomed to it.

As time passed on he began to talk, to hum, sing, scream, anything to create another sound, but it was always there, screaming in the background, hurting his ears, refusing to let him rest.

The noise was unrelenting. It was loud and hurt him as much as any physical blow. His skin was covered in scratches, made as he sunk his own short nails into his flesh in search of a distraction. He had heard of loud music being used to achieve this result, but never white noise. He was certain he would prefer a song, a tune, something his mind could process, something that made sense.

The static sometimes sounded like voices, whispering to him with words he couldn't quite hear. Sometimes he convinced himself he could hear music within, mentally singing along with desperation to songs he knew were never present.

He wasn't sure how long he had been here now. The shade of white in the cell never altered. Nothing changed except for the hour. It felt like weeks, months, but the slight stubble as he grated his chin across his shoulder to provide some kind of sensory response told him it had maybe been a day at most.

"Well?" Raiden knew he should recognise that voice, but all had blurred into nothing. He focused on the sound, something else that wasn't the white noise, something new. He wondered when he had been pulled back up to standing. He thought he'd been lying down a second ago.

"Nothing. Even vith this din, 'is mind is a steel trap. His lightning must somehow block my probing. Even vith the suppression bindings the pattern of 'is thoughts is erratic. I can make no sense of it." He focused on the voice, on the serenade of the musical tones of something different. Just the slightest part of him began to wonder what he would tell her if she promised to turn off the noise. But even that part of him would guard Maya, but the secrets he could spill. The things they didn't know about him. But those thoughts were sacred too, sealed in another vault, protected. They would never leave his lips without his consent.

He hoped.

He was beginning to question that, though. Question what he would give them for a second of peace.

"Ha," Raiden heard himself say, or at least he thought it was his voice. He tried to find the source of the voices, but his surroundings warped and twisted.

"Then let him stew." That was Mr Thorne, he was almost certain now those clipped words had belonged to him. "I have seen many driven to madness on white noise and lack of sleep, perhaps that will loosen his lips. By the time we have finished with him, the only thing he'll be good for is feeding from, but we'll have the girl."

"The girl," Raiden muttered. "Maya, sweet Maya." Fuck, he'd recognised that slurred voice, it was his own. Why was he talking? The room spun around him. Was he in a room? It seemed like nothing but open space, wide open whiteness as far as his eyes could see. He began to feel dizzy as nausea assailed him.

"Do you want to tell us where you hid her?"

"Storms and starlight," he muttered, smiling as he imagined her fingers teasing through his hair, pushing the locks from his eyes. He leaned back into the imaginary touch, ignoring the bite of the shackles at his wrist. Even here she could be his strength. "I missed you." He saw her smile in his mind, felt the warmth of her breath on his neck. "What are you doing here?" That touch was real, what would they do if they realised she was there, standing right behind him?

"Blaze, I'm so scared." He pressed his eyes closed tighter. Was that really her voice he heard? He felt her hand caress his shoulders, rubbing his burning limbs with gentle pressure.

"Maya," he groaned weakly, relishing the warmth of her touch. Warmth, but no sparks. What he would give to feel the sparks. Wait, what was it she had said, something wrong, something he couldn't quite remember.

"Where am I, Blaze?" Her fingernails gently scratched his stubble. Had she let them grow? No, Maya never let her nails grow. She kept them short, always short.

"You're safe, stay behind me, they'll never find you." He managed to glare towards the hand that slipped around him to stroke his chest, almost finding focus on Luiza's blurred features behind him.

"Soon, soon he will tell us where she is," said Mr Thorne. "Then we can break her slowly. His final punishment for his betrayal will be to force him to watch as we extinguish her spark. That is, if he can even understand what is happening. Tomorrow, bring the needles. Just a little something for him to look forward to."

~

The closer Maya got to the ambulance station, the more at ease she began to feel. Light rain filled the air, clinging to every surface, giving the streets an almost mystical glow while creating beautiful orbs of lights and halos around the streetlights. By the time she could see her car her brisk walk had become a sprint. Her vision fixed upon it, counting the remaining steps. Her low work shoes thumped against the dark pavement as her fingers clutched tightly to her keyring, her fingers upon the small panic alarm until she felt her arm being wrenched, twisted back with such force it sent them flying from her grasp.

"I was wondering when you'd show up." Rick's arm snaked around her waist as he pressed himself against her from behind. She thrust her head back, hoping to daze him, but he was too tall, her blow did nothing but make him chuckle.

"Let go."

"Oh no, you see, some very important people are going to pay me a lot of money to take you to them." Maya strained against him, screaming, screaming as loud as she could until she felt the coarse fabric of a rag smothering her nose and mouth. "They already took your latest fuck. Breathe deeply. I'm sure you'll be reunited soon. The Thorne family don't fuck around, but they do pay well." She held her breath, recognising the sweet taste as chloroform. There was no way he knew how to administer this properly. He'd probably seen it in some old television show and thought he'd give it a try.

She fought against him, her chest burning for a breath as she closed her eyes, letting her struggles still, before going limp in his arms. She'd let him drag her to the car. Then, when he needed to release her to get her inside, she'd make her move. As she predicted, as soon as she stopped resisting, he removed the cloth. She could feel the dizziness from the small amounts she had inhaled. But she could do this. Despite her burning need to breathe, she tried to keep her breathing slow. She'd only have one chance.

"What the hell is going on here?" Damn it, Maya knew that voice. Mike. She felt a little dazed as she slid from Rick's grasp to the pavement. Although she had not inhaled much, it was enough to be disorientating. It took a moment for her mind to register that Mike had punched Rick, and the shrill screaming in her ears was his panic alarm blaring.

Rick moved, catching Mike with a lucky blow on his chin as Maya struggled to her feet, watching him go down. Her fingers fumbled with her belt, freeing the concealed tranquiliser dart. Rick was kicking Mike in the ribs, another blow for good measure, a blow that meant he hadn't realised she was up, not until he felt the sharp scratch of the dart as she plunged it deep into his neck.

He spun around, grasping her throat weakly, thrusting her against the car as the drugs began to take effect. Now that was how you knocked someone out. Forget chloroform. This was foolproof. Luckily Rick didn't have the same insight she did.

"You bitch," he slurred.

"Where's Raiden?" she demanded as his grasp weakened slightly, his knees trembling. She needed answers, and quickly, there wasn't long left. She could hear the rapid approach of footsteps closing in, her mind finding it difficult to comprehend that everything that had just happened had taken place in mere seconds.

The report of a tranquiliser gun rang through the air as another brightly coloured fletching appeared in his back. He looked up to her, flashing a twisted, bloody-toothed smile that sucked all the heat from her.

"Dead." She heard his body hit the floor as her legs began to tremble.

"Bambi, hey, Bambi, you with us?" She was on her knees, Mike crouched before her, his own panic alarm silencing. "Thank goodness you carry that dart. You'd think I'd know to keep my glass jaw shielded. It's why I never made it as a boxer in school."

She could see his eyes, filled with concern as he rubbed his hands up and down her arms quickly, trying to force some warmth into her cold body. "Hey, Bambi, it's okay." He pulled her to his chest, still rubbing her until someone draped something over her shoulders. Even then he continued trying to share his warmth.

Dead. Raiden was dead.

She'd just found him. She couldn't lose him, not again. It was only as she felt the warmth of Mike's arms around her she realised she was shaking.

"The Blue Coats will be here any second, why don't you take her inside. We'll keep an eye on this piece of shit." The curse word was punctuated by something that sounded distinctly like a foot to the ribs.

"Hey, Bambi, come on, talk to me."

She suddenly realised she was sitting in the common room, her knees hugged to her chest and the weight of multiple blankets pressing down over her shoulders. She could hear everything that was going on around her and was even mostly aware of movement that passed before her unfocused gaze. The light shining in her eyes, a device beeping in time with her rapid pulse, a prick to her finger. She was aware of it all, but none of it seemed to register.

"How's she doing?" she heard Station Officer Silvers ask. Given that she didn't hear a reply, she imagined Mike must have shook his head. It wasn't that she didn't want to speak, she wanted to answer, to tell him she was fine, just a little shaken, but her voice just didn't work. She wasn't sure her lips even moved. "Is there anyone we can call?"

"I tried to get her friend Carley, but I got voicemail, she's out of town for the week."

"Do you know how much of a dose she got?"

"Not much, I saw her go down. I was only out for a few seconds, so for her to be up, I think she was putting on a show for him."

She closed her eyes, seeing the bloody teeth smiling at her, hearing his voice. *Dead,* the word mocked her. It had been delivered with such cold indifference, yet it had possessed the power to destroy her world. Mike seemed to be looking through her device, seeing if there was anyone else he could call.

"Well, we've always known Bambi's a smart girl. The Blue Coats have hauled him off. Did you recognise him?"

"Her ex, Rick."

"Hey, what about that Blaze guy, the one who dropped by the other day. Has anyone tried to reach him?"

"Raiden." She heard her voice, a whisper. She blinked, becoming more connected with her surroundings.

"What's that, Bambi?" Mike crouched before her. She knew he'd heard the name, the name of the person everyone had insisted was nothing more than a fantasy. The people here had never said anything, but she had seen their expressions when she accidentally let his name slip in the past. Unlike her former colleagues, they were simply too respectful to say anything, even behind her back.

"Raiden was here?" Her voice was a little louder this time. Her hand darted out to grasp Mike's arm so quickly the blankets slid from her back.

"Who?"

"Blaze. Raiden Blaze." This time it was her

S.O. who came into view, crouching down beside her partner. She watched the way the lights above reflected on his greying hair as she waited for his answer.

"He wanted to follow up on the Blue Coat's investigation. I'm not sure why the P.T.F. are involved, but he said he was taking a personal interest in your case. He was worried someone was going to try to hurt you. He thought someone was watching the building."

Maya lifted her device from Mike's hand, finding a picture of him she'd taken while he was sleeping. "Yeah, that's him." Tears brimmed her eyes. *Dead.* The blood-stained teeth goaded in her mind. She held back her shudder.

"When."

"About three days ago." Releasing Mike, she took a quick glance around, reconfirming she was still where she thought she was.

"I have to go." He was here three days ago, just before he went to the cemetery. Rick said he was dead, but what if he wasn't, what if he was alive, what if they'd buried him alive, and even now his air was running out? That's what those kind of families were known for, slow torturous deaths or quick executions. Where better to hide a body than a place full of them?

The beeping from the device near her sped

up as her pulse began to race. She had to get out of there. There was still hope. And if he was dead then who better to bring him back than a necromancer? She needed answers, and she wasn't going to sit around here waiting for them.

"Bambi, the Blue Coats are going to want to talk to you about what just happened." Mike kept his eye contact with her firm, maintaining it even when she glanced away.

"Trust me, the Blue Coats don't want to know." Everyone knew that there were some who were willing to look the other way where the crime families were involved. People had weaknesses, they were corruptible.

"Detective Reuben is already on his way."

"It'll just delay me. Tell them I'm unconscious or something, buy me some time, please." She glanced around, looking for her keys. Mike grasped her hand, placing them in her palm but not letting go.

"Bambi, are you in danger?" Mike questioned. She could hear Station Officer Silvers talking to someone quietly on his device. He kept glancing towards her, his concern evident.

"No, just my ex playing mind games," she lied and knew from his expression he didn't buy her answer for one second.

"And the photos?" Mike prompted. "Do you think Rick could be involved with Pyre-starter, could he be Pyre-starter?"

"He sent them." She saw the look on Mike's face and silently begged him not to say anything, aware that even though her S.O. was on a call, he was listening to their every word. Mike clearly remembered she had told him Rick had no idea what she did for a living. His gaze held hers for several long seconds before he released his grasp on the keys, but he still barred her retreat when she stood. "Please, I need to clear my head. I'll see them tomorrow."

"At least tell me where are you going?"

"The cemetery."

"Why?"

"To see my dad. I need to think. Please, Mike, Sir." She moved her gaze between them. "I need to do this, and they've already taken Rick into custody. Surely waiting to take my statement until morning won't cause any problems."

"Alright, Bambi. I'll buy you thirty minutes, then I'm not only telling them you sneaked out, I'm telling them where you went."

She wanted to negotiate for longer but knew better than to push her luck. Mike knew she was lying; she had to accept his compromise. "Thank you."

He stepped aside, meeting their S.O.'s gaze as she, only a little unsteadily, slipped away through the side door.

CHAPTER 14

*R*aiden's head pounded, his stomach clenching violently. He lay curled up on the floor in the foetal position, his shackled wrists pushed into his chin so his fingers could press down on his ears. But still he could hear the white noise. It permeated everything. He could even feel its vibrations across the floor, the floor which had no real feeling to it, it felt the same as everything else in this room, as if it was made on nothingness, neither hot nor cold. There were times he couldn't tell if he was lying down or suspended.

His captor hadn't visited for a while, not since he had seen through her attempts to make him think she was Maya. She could never be

Maya. He was almost certain that the times she visited were punctuated with him being suspended, when she left they lowered him back to the floor, sometimes.

He was supposed to consider this a mercy, a measure of dignity. Despite his attempts, he couldn't slow his rapid breathing, his racing heart. He could no longer stand due to the overwhelming dizziness. The room around him spun as if he were drunk. Everything hurt, his brain hurt, his muscles hurt, even his hair hurt.

The nauseating spinning made him want to vomit, but there was nothing to come up. They allowed him just enough water a day to ensure they could continue this torture, but he wasn't sure how much longer his body could endure. Perhaps that would be a relief, but if he were to fade, who would protect Maya?

It wasn't until he felt the chair beneath him he realised that the harsh and nauseating sensations had been from movement. Two large thugs, completely adorned in white, of course, stood either side of him, releasing the shackles holding his wrists to the arms of the chair as they wrapped thick leather straps around him. This would have been the perfect opportunity to call on his lightning, stun them and escape. They'd removed the suppressors, but they'd also known he was too weak to summon any resistance, let alone command the storm within.

"You should just tell me vhere she is, save yourself some pain." Raiden's unfocused gaze found her. In her hand was a white cloth roll. He knew what was to come, yet she made a display of slowly unrolling it, placing it on a small white collapsible table she brought in with her. Within this room everything simply became background. The table vanished from his gaze the moment he blinked.

The only thing not lost to an endless sea of white was the thin bamboo needles. She passed each one, all ten, before his blurred gaze before placing them on the table. "Vhere is she?" Despite his exhaustion, his faltering grasp on what was real and what visions only danced within his mind, Raiden clenched his jaw. His heart quickened further still. Fast, shallow beats. He cried out as the needle was placed between his nail and fingertip. She pressed it slowly, her face a testament to how much she savoured this moment.

"Fuck you," he growled weakly, trying to breathe. Her laugh sent ice chasing across his flesh, but it did little to numb the agony that one small needle caused.

"Vhen ve find her, I vill be the one breaking

her. I vill not show her the same kindness I 'ave you. She vill suffer for more your insubordination, and I vill 'ave you vatch. Her screams will serenade you night and day, and you vill listen, knowing you could do nothing to 'elp her, knowing you are the cause of her extra torment." Another scream, another needle, not quite far enough to begin loosening the nail, but perfectly inserted to cause the most pain.

He knew she was being careful, meticulous, after all. She didn't want to remove the nails too soon, that would spoil her fun. She was skilled in torture, she could draw this one out for days, maybe weeks, and it never got any less painful. "I vill go easier on her if you tell me vhat I vant to know." She grasped his face between her slender fingers, lifting his hanging head so he had no choice but to look at her.

"I'll not tell you. No one touches what is mine. Not even you."

"Pity." She smiled coldly, taking another needle.

Raiden wasn't sure how much time passed, but it dragged by in pain and exhaustion. There were times he blacked out, only to be roused by ice-cold water. Each of his fingers had small needles embedded within them, each one a source of unrelenting pain, impossibly heightened further with each gentle press and twist. He had never known something so simple could hurt so much, that it was possible to feel this much pain. Just when he thought it was impossible for things to hurt any more, she proved to him how wrong he was. Each fresh escalation of agony was met with the same question, and at the times when he could muster the breath, he told her where to go.

"Madam." He would like to say he relaxed when he heard the voice, but even without her measured touch, the agony never dulled. He tried to focus on the voice that intruded, hear what was so important that someone dared to interrupt her fun. "That maggot Rick has reported he is about to apprehend the reaper."

"Very good, prepare the cage. Vell, Mister Blaze, time is up. Looks as if ve are done 'ere." The smile turning her lips was born in hell itself. "I vonder if she'll be as challenging as you. There are so many vays to break a voman. I vill destroy her slowly. After all, ve need her functioning. Obedient, but functioning. I cannot vait to 'ear her screams, I vonder if they vill be as sweet as yours. You should never 'ave crossed my family. Get comfortable, Blaze, I still 'ave plans for you, but first you shall 'ear her beg for death."

"Don't you touch her," he growled with alarming strength.

"I vill be doing more than touching."

He strained against the restraints, a new vigour rising within him. Each movement further heightened his pain, but he had to get free, he had to protect her. "You said she was yours. It appears you vere mistaken, now she is mine." The door closed behind her as she left. The silence seemed all-consuming as he fought weakly. Silence, he realised. The white noise that had haunted him was gone, and part of him knew the next sounds he heard would be Maya's screams.

"Fuck." He wanted to yell the words, but they came out as nothing more than a hoarse whisper constricted by a throat swollen by pain and fear.

Maya pulled her car to a halt outside the cemetery. The mist-like rain appeared like a blanket of fog while the strong winds whipped across the tombs, carrying the small particles with it in an eerie motion that spoke of creatures moving in the mists. Maya's hands rarely shook, a trained response to being a surgeon, but they did now. The low lighting from her device showed her as a blinking dot, and somewhere within the mass of graves was another.

Her fingers wrapped around the bars of the intimidating wrought iron gates, thrusting them inward, as if hoping the silver chain she saw securing them was nothing more than decoration. She knew this wasn't the case; she had visited here a lot in the nighttime after her father's death.

The cemetery in Overton closed at sunset. No exceptions. She had once arrived in time to see the grounds-keeper scattering the pine needles across the path, fortifying the natural defences. Most people would turn back, but anyone who had ever visited knew that just three railings up, hidden by the foliage of the evergreen shrubs that grew beneath one of the many pine trees, the bars had been bent, allowing many daredevil teenagers—or witches seeking rare flowers that only bloomed at night upon the graves of kindred spirits—to slip inside for a quiet night of mischief.

With pine trees surrounding the entire graveyard, there was no chance creatures spawned of dark intentions, or beings tethered to the tombs of the dead, could leave. The moment such entities touched the needles, the shielding sustaining their forms would be pierced. Nothing incorporeal or of ill intent could cross pine needles.

Maya pushed her slender figure through the railings, squirming as her body protested the narrow gap. She could have sworn it was much larger when she had last used this secret entrance. Branches snagged in her ponytail, tugging at her hair as if the shrubbery was a gatekeeper warning her back. But there was no going back, not if there was the slightest chance Raiden was alive, and if he was dead, well, she'd address that when the time came.

Death was no longer permanent.

Either way, she needed to look, to see for herself. If she was going to lose herself for someone, it would be him. Perhaps the necromancers in the old horror movies had been misunderstood too. Perhaps their tales had also started out as love stories. Perhaps, along the way, they traded their soul for another's, accepting a darkness to return a light.

The fine mists clung to her skin, penetrating her clothes in a way that only this type of weather could. Her unguarded steps left deep impressions, bending the sodden, overgrown grass to her will as she strode forwards with her device in hand, watching the map update, watching herself get closer with every step she took. He wasn't far now. Her mind warned her of the need for caution, yet her feet carried her on without heeding such advice.

Of course it would be a mausoleum, she thought to herself, standing before the large crypt entrance. It wasn't gated, or even sealed, just a large marble building with an enormous gaping mouth descending one step at a time into darkness. With a deep breath she walked down, wondering what the hell she was thinking. The lower she descended, the more she doubted her plan, or lack thereof. It was becoming painfully apparent this was not a place for honouring the dead, or at least honouring the dead who no longer walked.

As she reached the bottom, a hall extended before her. Magical fire burned in ancient sconces, enhancing the Gothic atmosphere while playing in the deep shadows of the carved marble walls. Each flicker of flame gave the impression of movement.

Her stomach twisted painfully as she passed the first of many detailed stone doors. She kept her footfall as quiet as possible, but she did not walk with the whisper of the dead. If her boots did not betray her presence, then surely the loud pounding of her heart would announce her to any predators who could be lurking.

She swallowed past the rising fear, her hands still trembling as she lifted the device. Her dot was just feet from his now. She stopped before the stone door. Ancient symbols seemed to have been engraved with a modern flair. She couldn't read this script, causing her to wonder if they were some manner of enchantment, a prison, a trap, a sanctuary? There was only one way to find out.

Reaching out she felt the stone door give beneath her gentle push. She held her breath, almost expecting, hoping, to see Raiden within the dimly lit room. But instead of her god crafted from storms and starlight, she saw a being of pure darkness. His black irises seemed magnified through his thick-rimmed glasses as he looked up and hissed. For a second Maya couldn't believe she'd actually heard that sound as his fangs hinged forwards in his jaw like a snake.

"Well, well, well, what do we have here, is someone a little lost?" He tossed a device to the desk, the glow of countless monitors causing his thick black hair to possess a blue sheen. It didn't take her many seconds to understand what she was looking at, why Raiden's device was here. The room was filled with electronics, the kind she had seen once before in a store when she had tried to recover the data from her father's fried computer. Whoever this vampire was, he was trying to gain access to whatever information Raiden had stored on there. Which begged the question, if his device was here, where was Raiden?

"I-I," she stammered as a plan formulated in her mind. She pulled her hair free from its bindings, shaking her head slightly so it swayed under the power of her movements. Arching her back, she thrust her chest forward, lifting a finger to tease her lips. "I heard there was a crypt."

She traced her fingers across her cheek, brushing her hair aside as she tilted her head, swaying backwards on her heels as if she were drunk. "I heard," she whispered huskily, tugging the neckline on her low-cut tank top, ensuring her chest heaved knowing his gaze was divided between studying her cleavage and her throat. Men, even vampire men, were more often than not predictable. They had the same base desires and often less restraint.

"Oh, what did you hear?" He stalked towards her, flinging the desk aside in a display of strength as he removed all barriers between them. He was before her in a second, running a finger across her jaw. She closed her eyes, forcing out a soft moan.

"That being bitten is..."

"Like an orgasm, a powerful, all-encompassing orgasm," he finished for her. "Would you like me to give you a taste?"

Maya licked her lips, nodding, praying. "But what I actually heard," she whispered breathlessly, closing her eyes as she felt it, the prickle of energy across her skin, the heat building up within her core, "was that you were going to take me to Raiden Blaze."

"What?" He recoiled from her, seeming dazed but not compliant. She thought back to the feelings she had when she had commanded the dead back to life, forced a stilled heart to beat, a body to move, and at once, she knew what was missing. Confidence. They had obeyed her because there was no choice, she hadn't asked them, she'd demanded it. She told them what was expected, and they obeyed.

"I said," she repeated with more power behind her voice, "take me to Raiden Blaze." She would never be able to put into words the feelings that encompassed her in that moment. It was as if his body knew it belonged to her, his essence recognised he was hers to command. His dead bones obeyed and his spirit surrendered to her.

It was a powerful sensation as his will bent to hers, one that chased through her like a raw jolt of electricity. Every cell in her body felt charged, and the longer she was in control, the more powerful she felt. She bit her lip as she felt the vitality being drawn from him to empower her as he surrendered all that he was to her command. Body, mind, and soul, and with each passing second, she craved more of his strength.

It was addictive, it was sustenance, and she was hungry, starving.

She wanted more, needed more.

Her body and soul relished in the feeling. It made her feel almost complete, whole in a way different to being in Raiden's arms. Raiden. The thought of him was enough to break the spell, enough to steady her mind and not have her seeking new prey to bend to her will. She was here for him, only him.

"Yes, mistress." There was no resistance. She had expected a battle of wills, or a feeling of fatigue like that which assailed her when she brought people back. But instead there was just energy. Her whole body felt as if she was charged. The figure exited the room, guiding her silently through the winding corridors.

"What is this place?"

"It is where the Thorne family handles more discrete matters. It is also the location of their dungeon, mistress."

She shuddered as he answered, unsure if it was from the new surge of energy or the thought of the depravity that had occurred within these walls.

He brought them to a stop outside a heavy door. It was the first of many that possessed no carvings, no markings. Something about the way the door sat so snuggly against the wall was different to how the others had been mounted. He didn't let her study it for long. His hand was upon it, pushing it open, with such ease that for the briefest moment she questioned why it possessed no lock.

It was a question soon answered. It had no lock because the prisoner would never reach the door. The room within was white, so white it appeared as if the slumped figure, whose half-naked body was heartbreakingly bruised and bloody, was sitting upon thin air.

Her breath hitched painfully as she saw his gaunt waxy skin. He hadn't even moved at the sound of their arrival. It was all she could do not to rush to his side, to trace her hands over him and see if he drew breath. But she knew better than to trust her safety to a magic she didn't understand and a room that sealed so completely from the inside that no door would be visible.

"Retrieve him," she commanded. Her servant's heavy footsteps became silent as he marched across the threshold with purpose. "Gently." As he obeyed, another bristle of energy chased across her flesh. She watched as Raiden was unstrapped from the chair. Even with it at his back, Raiden collapsed forwards into his rescuer's embrace, his feet trying to walk as if by instinct.

Maya gasped, seeing the small needles protruding from his fingertips and, as her vampire supported his weight, she carefully removed them, his weakened whimpers breaking her heart. She needed to hold him, to feel him in her arms. She took him from the thug. Placing his arm around her shoulders as she leaned forward, trying to shift his weight to her back.

"Help me." Knowing what was wanted of him, the vampire lifted Raiden on her back. Tucking her arms beneath his legs to keep him in place, she reached up to grasp his wrists. "Lead us out." Again her skin prickled as he complied. Raiden's weight was crushing, sweet torture. His shallow exhales against her skin gave her the strength to carry him, to put one foot before the other.

She was not a fighter. Raiden was in rough shape, so she was relying on her vampire to protect them should their paths cross with anyone else. She struggled with the weight, her feet dragging across the floor. He was heavy. She felt his weight bearing down upon her, the burn of her muscles. Yet at the same time, he weighed nothing. She could carry him forever and never falter.

Her knees buckled slightly as if challenging her mental resolve. *Mind over matter,* she told herself as she reached the ascending stairs. For a moment she wondered if she had the strength, but then by its own accord, her mind took her back to the paper she had written on polio and the article she had found on Boys Town. *He ain't heavy,* she asserted mentally as she adjusted his weight slightly. *He's my lover,* she added mentally, changing the symbolic words slightly as she began the climb.

By the time she felt the sweet kiss of the autumn wind she was covered in sweat, her limbs were shaking, and even the power of her connection to the vampire did little to alleviate her fatigue. They had reached the graveyard without incident, something that caused Maya's heart to race. She expected some confrontation, some challenge. She had barely taken her first staggering steps from the entrance of the crypt when she regretted the thought.

Tempting Providence, that was the phrase her father would have used.

CHAPTER 15

$\mathcal{M}$aya barely had time to register the small group awaiting them when something struck her. She wasn't sure what it was, but the force of her hitting the ground knocked the wind from her as both she and Raiden skid across the slick grass, leaving a trail of mud and debris in their wake. She tried to keep hold of him, but he slipped from her. She scurried across the ground towards him, but another figure reached him first, dragging his limp body away.

"Vhat did I tell you, she came right to us."

"Let him go!" she snarled, pushing herself up with her hands as she glared at the model like woman. "Protect him!" she screamed, searching for her servant, but where once he had stood naught but ashes remained.

"Oh, I'll let him go alright, into the next world." She smirked. "Vhat's the matter, are we making the little reaper cry?"

Maya could feel her tears mingling with sweat as they tracked a path down her flushed cheeks. Rage simmered within her, her temperature beginning to spike.

"Don't."

"Or what?"

"You think I came to your domain?" Maya whispered, tears of anger growing hotter as her rage boiled. "But you're in mine. You wanted the power of a necromancer, well. Here. I. Am." She dragged herself to her feet, her mud-streaked clothing sticking to her flesh, her damp hair tangled, hanging limply around her shoulders.

She looked anything but threatening, and yet she beheld the uncertainty in some of their eyes. "If you don't release him, I'll give you a true taste of my power. I'll rain it down upon you." She was no longer crying, no longer trembling, she was simply angry. Filled with a rage so hot it became cold as it flooded through her veins, her skin prickled with electricity as each enraged breath drew more energy into her. This was what true anger felt like, true rage. "My domain is endless, and we stand amongst millions of my allies. Try me, I dare you."

"You're bluffing, you are naught but a fledgling." There was fear in the woman's voice, uncertainty.

"Release him," Maya growled, her eyes snapping to the figure who held Raiden. His obedience was instant, sending Raiden tumbling to the ground. A fresh surge of energy powered through her, making her stand taller, stronger. She was a goddess amongst these fools, and no one touched what was hers.

They would bow down to serve her or be destroyed.

"I am still a mistress of death, and each one of you belongs to my domain."

"Kill him." The woman shrugged.

Maya felt the energy roll from her fingers, paralysing everyone within the grasp of her extending aura. She concentrated on the figures who tried to move, reached out with her dominance to bend them to her will, prevent the advance of those who had turned towards Raiden.

He was hers.

Power thrummed through her veins, seducing her, whispering to her promises of more. Not everyone was ensnared. There were beings here so old they needed a show of true strength to be brought to heel. The woman and another remained standing while their servants became hers, dropping to their knees.

Her heritage whispered through her veins, telling her what she must do, guiding her exploration of the magic she unlocked, teaching her to wield it. She felt her power swelling, the connection to the dark realm strengthening.

Her gaze was so focused on the threat of the woman she failed to see the man advance. Lightning quick, his fist connected with her stomach. Before the pain exploded, she found herself once more face down in the dirt. Her delicate hold on the tendrils of energy slipped.

Groaning, she turned over, attempting to grasp the escaping threads. She needed to concentrate, something the pain radiating through her did not allow. She needed to block it out, push it aside for later. Focus on what needed to be done, like she did every day when her job became chaotic.

Despite the fact Maya could see the woman's heels sinking deep into the sod as she approached, never once did her steps falter. The woman glided gracefully towards her until Maya's hair was tangled within her fist wrenching her to her knees while her partner effortlessly turned his own comrades, the beings still held within her control, to ash as he advanced upon Raiden.

"You vill learn this is your place. On your knees before me. You'll vant to vatch this, little reaper. Did you really think you could 'old more than two of us vithout training? Did you think you could 'old me?"

She heard Raiden groan as he was dragged to his knees. The sound was sweet agony, confirming he lived, that he was conscious, but warning his remaining breaths could be counted in seconds.

His eyes opened for the first time, his beautiful ice-blue eyes immediately meeting hers and flooding with such emotion, such terror, it caused her throat to swell.

His head dropped, hanging in defeat as a bead of moisture upon his face sparkled, tracing the contour of his cheek like a tear. They wrenched his head backwards He closed his eyes, another crystal tracking his cheek as a sharp talon was placed to his throat.

"Don't," she whispered.

"No, make it slow." The command was spoken with a cruel smile.

"Please, I'll do anything," she begged, her hands gripping the woman's thighs. "Please."

"I vant her to remember his every fading breath."

Maya felt the warmth of Raiden's presence through the bracelet on her wrist as her heart began to race. No. This wasn't how this would end. *She* was the mistress of death, and right now she could feel the call of the dead offering her their aid, offering to deliver a vengeance that would bring the world to its knees.

A surge of energy jolted through the bracelet, empowering her as the soft earth at her knees began to feed the growing heat within her. The first drop of crimson that puckered on his flesh undid her. She didn't reach for the energy, she snatched it, claiming it for her own, drinking it in hungrily.

"Stop!" she demanded, and they did. The hulking colossal finger whose nail had just barely broken Raiden's skin froze. The woman whose hand was tangled in her matted hair froze. Their dead bones, their expired spirits, all obeying as their energy mingled with her own, feeding her, granting her strength and control.

The power surged again. "Release me." The fingers unthreaded from her hair. She could still feel her resistance, her will trying to overpower the instinct to obey. Another surge washed over Maya, a mere swell compared to the tsunami that she felt approaching. She drank it in, wave after wave, each one making her stronger, more powerful than the last, quashing any resistance she had felt.

The sound of the dead, the bones sleeping beneath the ground, she could hear them all as her awareness spread, extending the touch of her aura across the graves of the fallen. All of them called to her, screaming for her to command them, to let them empower her, let them please her and channel to her the energies from the land of the dead.

"Kneel," she commanded, the dull impact of not just the two figures she knew of, but three others who had been hiding in the shadows, collapsing to their knees serenaded her. Their compliance rippled over her, rewarding her and enhancing the restless cries of those wanting to be liberated to serve their mistress.

The power washing over her was addictive. She wanted more, needed more, and as she devoured each wave, the tsunami from below drew closer. She was starving, and the dead provided a link to the powers of the underworld, a sustenance she never knew she needed, and now she had fully touched it, she was ravenous, insatiable. She needed more.

Raiden's energy bristled through her, adding

flames to the fire of her rage. She heard the elation leave her lips as spectral forms began to rise, surrounding her in their ethereal protection against any unseen foes, promising to bring more souls to command, more power, a torrent of the dead, each opening more pathways to channel that which her soul craved.

Sparks akin to Will-o'-the-Wisps danced in her wild eyes as the voices sang to her, asking who were her enemies, how could they please her, how could they serve her. She licked her lips. Who were her enemies? She could scarcely remember, what did she want? She wanted more. More of this feeling. More of this power. More dead to sustain her.

"Maya," she heard Raiden's voice, a mere whisper amongst the worship that empowered her. At her feet the ground began to tremble. Those once put to rest stirred, rising to protect their mistress from any who would dare cross her, dare try to stop her from fully opening the gateway between the two realms.

The dead serenaded her, raising her arms she began to sway, understanding now why dance had always called to her, why ancient shamans and tribesmen danced, it was empowering, a ritual. She had never felt more alive than now the dead rose to serve her.

She would erase her enemies, she would claim their souls, bind them to her, have them serve her for eternity as she claimed this beautiful land as her own and brought her armies from the shadows of hell. She would claim them all, the souls of her enemies, of every living thing. After all, the living had no purpose, they would all be better, happier, under her control. They would know no pain, no death, only the joy of being bound to her. The world held too much pain, now it was time to be free of such burdens.

Never again would there be the pain of holding a loved one, of watching them slip away. Never again would people kill one another, threaten each other. Her world would be one of peace, one where people were free to love one another without fearing for their lives. One where she and Raiden could be together.

She felt shaking hands come to rest upon her hips, a sensation that caused a different charge to chase across her skin, another surge of energy, different yet just as empowering. She was unstoppable, she could rule the world, and everyone who fell would rise again, bow to her, serve her. She was their mistress, tamer of the darkness, holder to the gates of the underworld and mortal remains.

There was not a force that could stand against her. Not the Thorne family, not disease and illness. Not even death.

The feeling was intoxicating. She grasped the hands, absorbing the electricity of his presence as she swayed in time with the music of the damned.

Command us mistress, what is your bidding? Bind us, use us, let us please you. Let us bring death to the living so they may serve you.

Alex arrived at the ambulance station just in time to see Detective Mendel's shoulders heave in a sigh. In all honesty, he knew how the man felt. Since they had discovered the existence of a reaper, he had been placed at the Blue Coat's disposal.

He ran a hand through his hair, smiling to himself. It was the most natural gesture in the world, that was, unless someone perceived him as being bald. It had happened before, he'd passed it off as an old habit, but since then he tried to avoid such tells. He could never be sure what someone else saw when looking at him. That was why he had been sent as liaison. No one could ever really identify him.

There was a part of him that was happy to be so involved, but his love had always been his work beyond the barrier with the team he had trusted his life to more times than he could count. He was looking forward to getting back out there, but for now, his sister needed him, and he had already disappointed her more than any older brother should. He hadn't been there when she needed him, but he was going to be there now, and if that meant he was assigned the occasional seek-and-recover mission, then so be it.

His orders had been none specific, bordering on vague. He was to attempt to bring the target in alive so the P.T.F. could uncover what her motives were, but if there was the slightest hint of a threat he was to neutralise her. Despite Perennials being protected species, reapers were too dangerous to allow them free rein.

The problem was, no one had ever controlled a reaper, they had an endless supply of forces at their beck and call. They were quick to become berserkers, and once they let the darkness in there was no hope of controlling them. It was only thanks to Detective Mendel that they had pieced together her identity. If not for him asking for the living corpse of Fredrick McArther to be diverted into their care they never would have realised the danger that walked their island, or that the serial killer, Pyrestarter, was actually not the villain they had been made out to be.

He had been warned to approach this mission with care. Reapers were volatile, easily corruptible, and almost unstoppable. There was death everywhere, and that was precisely what they fed on, the power of death, the energy of being its master, or in Maya Jarrett's case, its mistress.

The general consensus was this woman was raising an army, placing them back in their normal lives ready to answer her call when the uprising began. But something about that assessment had not sat well with Alex. It had seemed more an assumption woven by fear than a deduction created by facts. Yes, reapers in the past had been portrayed as evil creatures, but very little was actually known about them, especially since the last line of reapers sacrificed their lives along with the other Perennials. In his book, such an act of self-sacrifice did not come naturally to creatures who thrived on chaos and devastation.

He was determined to bring her in peacefully. He had been sent to retrieve her, a team was on standby, but he had insisted on entering alone, talking to her first. There was no reason to go in heavy-handed and guns blazing.

"Alpha Ciele, it's a pleasure to meet you again." Reuben extended his hand, setting the tone for their meeting. The formality indicated he had a similar doubt about this young woman. Something weighed on his shoulders. This ifrit had spoken to Maya personally and had not felt anything. No ties to the underworld, no tethers to undead souls. Nothing that would suggest she was the threat they perceived. And yet she'd also raised the dead, something an ifrit should have been able to feel.

"Detective Mendel." Alex acknowledged, pumping the offered hand a few times before glancing towards the small reception area, noticing that it was unmanned. The low-level lightning suggested it was a place that saw limited use in the evening hours. The entire foyer was empty, silent but for the low hum of a vending machine that was long overdue for a refill.

"You were updated on the way, I trust?"

"Indeed. But something has changed." Alex observed, referring to the almost hidden tension in the detective's shoulders.

"From what I understand, the reaper's ex-boyfriend attacked her in the car park, and she slipped out from observation about thirty minutes ago."

"Any thoughts as to where she was heading?" Alex felt a tingle of pressure between his shoulder blades. If she knew enough to run, to know that somehow they were on to her, then there was no telling what she would do.

"The cemetery."

"Please tell me you aren't serious."

"Deadly, if you'll excuse the pun." Alex had to resist the urge to groan. "I don't think this is as cut and dry as everyone seems to think. I've spoken to her, everyone who knows her says the same thing, she's a good person, smart, dedicated to her job."

"Do we have eyes on the target?" Alex pinched the bridge of his nose. Her running had complicated matters.

"Better than that, she's wearing a camera. I've transferred access to you." Alex heard his device beep as Reuben placed his own away.

"Okay, let's deploy to the cemetery. We can check the recordings on route and see what our little necromancer is scheming."

"What are our orders?"

"Target is to be brought in alive if possible, but the slightest hint of trouble, we shoot to kill. We can't be caught in a battle of the undead."

"You can't be serious! You're not really going out there to shoot Bambi?" Alex turned to see a blond-haired man standing in the doorway to the main station, having overheard the end of their conversation. "Tell me you're not serious. She's the sweetest kid I know, wouldn't hurt a fly." Alex recognised the man from his briefing; his name was Mike, Maya's part-time shift partner.

"I'm afraid details are classified."

"Classified my ass. Whatever you think she's done, I can guarantee you she hasn't. You didn't see her after Rick attacked her. She was terrified. The only thing that brought her out of the shock was the mention of her boyfriend, you should know him." The man gestured towards Alex's dark blue uniform. "He came by claiming to be P.T.F." Mike placed himself between Alex and the door.

"Do you have a name for this supposed P.T.F. member? I have been assigned to the case personally and have no mention of anyone else taking an interest."

"He's her boyfriend, Raiden Blaze."

"Blaze, as in the Thorne family Blaze?" Detective Mendel interrupted. "If they're an item then we've just discovered her motive. We're looking at a power-play."

"Alex Ciele?" A voice questioned behind

him. Turning, he saw a man with strawberry-blond hair, wearing a similar uniform to his own. "I am Roger, I have been asked to accompany you on your assignment. I have information that is pertinent."

Alex nodded, gesturing towards the exit. Time was a luxury they could not afford.

"We'll take it from here." He advised, glancing back towards Detective Mendel. He gave a nod, gathering his belongings.

Everything had happened too quickly. Raiden's mind was still racing, still trying to piece together what had just happened.

He had wanted to help her, to keep her safe, but he had been held in place. Luiza had forgotten all notions of making him hear her scream. All she wanted now was to tame the reaper. That Maya had somehow found him, risked her life to retrieve him, provided Luiza the perfect starting place to begin her destruction. Him. A tear leaked from his eye. He was meant to protect her, not be the tool of her destruction.

He tried to comfort her, to mentally bridge the distance between them. He wanted to tell her it would be okay, that even in death he would never really leave her. He felt it the moment it happened. As the talon punctured the skin on his throat, the world around him became death cold, the plumes of each rapid breath escaping his lips alone as she drew his energy to her. His lightning, his ice, both boosted her power. Her commands rang out as she seized control of the forces so easily accessible in the cemetery. He felt as if he were both one with her and separate, the tether of his energy different to those she fed from, its effect different. While the dead sought to unfasten her inhibitions, his fought to anchor her.

He felt the power flowing through her veins, saw the sparks in her aura giving birth to Will-o'-the-Wisps as it expanded as if carried by the wind to encompass the land beyond his sight. The dead were pulled from their peaceful slumber. But there were so many, each wanting to serve her. Luiza's hands released Maya as she and the figure holding Raiden dropped to their knees, worshipping his goddess.

He knew now why necromancers were thought to be evil. He could feel her body's responses to the addictive power as easily as if it were his own hands she shuddered beneath. The more she drew on the world around her, the more he felt her power increase. With each swell, additional beings sought to tether themselves to her and feed her cravings.

He crawled towards her, barely able to stand on weakened legs. His hands grasped her hips, offering her his energy not because she needed more, but because if he didn't find a way to anchor her, she risked losing her soul to the darkness he could feel inhibiting her judgement.

He understood everything now.

When she had revived the dead before, she had done so from a place of love, of needing to help. It had been pure and, as such, her soul had touched only goodness. She paid for their return with her own exhaustion. But here her actions had been spurred by anger and fear, connecting her with a darker realm, one that would feed her only to consume her and turn it to its bidding. There were so many dark spirits wanting to serve, so much power, it all distorted her reality.

He could see her slipping away, entering a trance, a trance she may never be free of, a trance that was as dangerous to herself as it was to the living world. It was here she would lose herself.

He saw the P.T.F. team approach, their guns trained upon her. He raised a hand. She hadn't bound anyone to her fully yet, merely accepted the energy they freely offered and commanded old bones to obey and spirits to rise. He needed to stop this. He tried whispering her name, certain she had almost heard him.

Quietly he began to hum their song. Her hips began to sway to a different beat, one created by the soft tones of his voice. It was the first sign she had heard him, that their song was more powerful than the music of the dead who tried to seduce her into its service.

He felt her leaning into him, the dead stilling at his touch. His soft breath caused her flesh to pucker as he began to match her sway, his hands tracing her curves slowly, his touch not causing the earth to move but still at her feet. Her wild eyes fluttered closed as his voice gained volume. It was the only song he could sing. He'd had years of practice, years of missing her.

She turned, he matched her movements despite the protests of his exhausted limbs. The forms of the dead lost strength, his touch overpowering their tethers, her body craving him more than the power they fed her. The ghosts became wisps, almost invisible as she let her grasp on them fade. That he had this effect on her moved him in a profound way, making him aware of the full extent of his feelings for her, feelings so all-consuming the word *love* would only dilute it. There was no word to explain this emotion because no word existed that could capture the intensity and power of something so extraordinary.

"Leave with me now," he whispered as the fletching struck her. Her eyes flitted open in terror, her beautiful dark brown eyes, no longer consumed with blackness and soul embers. She was snatched from his grasp before he could talk, his body wrestled to the ground as he fought to reclaim her. He growled, breaking free of the hold with ease, putting the P.T.F. member on his back before struggling to stand.

He needed to get to Maya. The other members of the task-force ignored him, cuffing the vampires who were slowly gaining their bearings only to find themselves the captive of a new force. He stumbled towards the vehicles abandoned within the cemetery grounds, to the one he had seen them place her inside. Extending his hand, he used what little strength he had left to thrust the door from the person's hand, closing it before they could get in.

"Blaze," acknowledged the tall figure exhaling a sigh with such force it lifted his strawberry-blond fringe. He knew this man, Roger. Thank the gods he knew this man. "Don't do anything foolish." His amber eyes warned as he reached for the handle again, cracking the door.

"How did you know?" Raiden's hand slammed against the door, again, his weight leaning into it, stopping Roger from gaining access to the vehicle. It was still too early for Lewis to have placed the call.

"Belt." Roger gestured towards the back seat as if his words should spark some recognition. "Detective Reuben suggested she kept it on. You're lucky Lewis called when he did, or I may have missed briefing the Alpha. When he realised she'd ran from the hospital, we connected to her camera. Saw the whole thing."

"Then you'll know none of this was deliberate. She saved me." Raiden felt his knees buckle and fought to remain upright. He could not fall here. If he did he would never see her again.

"We've no choice, you know that." Roger's tone was almost apologetic.

"Put me in with her. My cover's blown anyway. I won't leave her again." He felt Roger's hand grip him, steadying him as his legs kept their earlier promise to give.

"Well, what you waiting for? Hop in." Raiden leaned against the car while Roger opened the door. "Nine years down the pan. Sucks to be you." Roger mocked.

"I think the boss would rather have me

secure the reaper than have her broken and turned against them. I would give it all up again before I let anyone touch her." Roger eyed him with something almost resembling respect. It was the first hint of such a thing he had seen from this man in the last three years. Although they had met but a handful of times since, normally, Lewis had handled him.

"You're in trouble, you know. I hope you've got a damn good reason you didn't flag her." There was a heavy silence as Raiden leaned back, his every effort forced into remaining conscious. "You look like shit, you sure you don't need medical?" Roger tossed a blanket into the back, but instead of draping it over his bare and bruised chest, Raiden tucked it around Maya, stroking her face.

"I'll live. She better had too."

CHAPTER 16

When Maya awoke she was in a small holding cell. The air was clean, cool but not uncomfortable as it touched her sore flesh. Her skin hurt, invisible burns danced across her flesh from the energy that had coursed through her, and with a flash of heat nausea rose in her stomach.

She turned her head, the pressure in her chest easing as she saw Raiden sitting on the bed at the opposite side of the cell. The way the thin mattress dipped, revealing the springs, confirmed it had to be as uncomfortable as the one she lay on. He was sat with his head cradled in his hands.

His bare chest had been wrapped with

bandages, covering the injuries she hadn't even had chance to see during his rescue. She had known he was badly hurt, so the fact he was sitting, with his gaze fixed towards the clean marble floor, allowed her heart to beat a little easier.

Her head pounded, every limb burning. She felt like she had gone ten rounds with a bulldozer and lost, so she closed her eyes, feigning sleep a while longer, part of her hoping she could return to slumber and wake elsewhere.

She knew the laws, what happened when a preternatural stepped out of line, and she had certainly done that. She wasn't even sure she knew how she'd done what she did. She could still see the army of the dead surrounding her, remember the pull and draw of their presence, the power, the temptation, the addiction as she craved more. She wasn't sure if she had hurt anyone but knew Raiden had pulled her back before the tsunami had hit.

The least she was looking at was imprisonment, the worst, death. Or perhaps she had that backwards. Perhaps death would be the mercy. And what of Raiden? Was he thought to be an accomplice? He was jailed with her like a common criminal. Him, a man who had spent his life working for the Thorne family, avoiding brushes with the law, had been apprehended because of her, because he wouldn't leave her. She had condemned him as much as herself.

"I'm sorry, Raiden," she whispered. The quiet of their cell was unforgiving to the words she had meant to only think.

"Maya." He breathed her name with such relief it caused tears to well in her eyes. He dropped to his knees, crawling the short distance between them, taking her hand in his, placing his forehead to it. "I was wondering when you'd wake. How are you feeling?"

"Like the dead." She gave an ironic chuckle. "You? Are you okay? Raiden, when I saw you, I was so scared." She pushed herself up, pulling her hand free to run it through his hair, caressing his face as he lifted his gaze to meet hers. His skin looked better, it had lost the almost waxy texture it had possessed in the white room, but the dark circles rimming his eyes told tales of fatigue that would take more than a good night's sleep to resolve.

"Not bad. Maya, about what happened—"

"I'm really sorry. I'll explain to them you had nothing to do with this, they'll have to let you go." She prayed it was true. Raiden had always been meticulous in keeping his activities for the Thorne family hidden, any evidence they'd had always went missing, he was a name, nothing more, they couldn't charge him for his name. Not a single person had ever identified him. "You shouldn't be in here with me. I'll find a way to keep you out of this. Did they... did they give any indication of their intentions?"

"I guess that's something we'll have to talk about. Are you thirsty?" He moved to sit beside her on the small bed.

She noticed the way he winced, how his muscles tensed as he moved. She had no doubt he was buffering his reactions. He'd been tortured. She wanted to undress the wounds, to see what she was dealing with, heal him with her own hands, but without anything at her disposal, she'd only make things worse. He reached slowly beneath the bed to retrieve a bottle of water, handing it to her. She stared at it, seeing the contrast of the clear fluids against the blackening of his fingernails. She grasped it at the bottleneck, ensuring her fingers did not brush against his and cause him any more pain.

"What were you thinking coming after me, and alone at that? Gods, Maya, do you know what they could have done to you?" He passed a hand through his hair, grimacing.

"I wasn't thinking. Rick told me you were dead, I had to find out. I had to know."

"You left the safe house," he scolded gently.

"You hadn't moved for days," she protested, placing her hand upon his wrist.

"And how would you know?"

"I put Tracking-Mate on your phone, I used it to find you." While she had been ashamed of her actions at the time, she could find that feeling no longer. Her breach of his privacy had saved him. She had saved him.

"Impossible, I factory reset it to avoid exposing you."

"It doesn't matter. It's a hidden safety app. It can't be removed unless I disconnect the tether." She looked towards the floor, watching the movement of her shadow as she swung her legs. "I'll clear all this up; you shouldn't be punished because I—I'll not fight whatever verdict, I'll keep my mouth shut, I'll cooperate fully without resistance, so long as they let you walk." She wasn't sure how she was going to achieve this. The only thing she could really offer them was to go down without a fight.

"Maya, they know what I was doing, they'll—"

"They'll understand. You only killed those people because they were already dead, because I'm, what, a necromancer, a reaper? You know, I don't think that I really believed you, not until I came across that vampire." She squeezed his knee as his intense gaze snapped to her in alarm. She found herself unable to hold his gaze and instead studied the coarse tile flooring.

"You mean you came to rescue me, and didn't have a plan?"

"Well..." A slight cringe accompanied her smile.

"Are you nuts?" He pushed himself, sucking in a breath. His every muscle tensed to the point she could see the bulging of his tendons as he moved, his vision now anywhere but on her. "Maya, how did you even know you could control the undead?"

"I used logic. You said I was a necromancer, necromancers raise the dead and summon spirits. Vampires are walking corpses with a spirit. I figured they'd obey me." It had been a shot in the dark, but it made sense. The science was there, the medical facts were there.

"How did you even do it?"

"Electricity?" she questioned, cringing slightly. "I don't really know, I—"

"You don't know? You didn't know if you could do it and you still—"

"I figured that if it was to save you, I could unlock anything. I was right, it's just I didn't expect it to be so..." She shuddered, rubbing her hands up and down her bare arms to chase away the creeping chill.

"Powerful?" He turned to face her at last, levelling her with a gaze that told her he both loved her and feared for her.

"Seductive," she confessed in a whisper. "Raiden, how I felt, the way my thoughts spiralled, it was like I couldn't think clearly anymore. If they gave me the death penalty it would be justified." She sighed, twirling one of her tangled locks around her finger. "I want you to know if that's what happens, I'm okay with it."

"Don't say that." There was a quiet emotion in his voice, one which caused her heart to swell. It wasn't anger, but it had all its markers. The difference was it was softer, more intimate. It was the combination of many things, of love, fear, and rage being portrayed in a whisper so powerful even the deaf would hear it.

"You didn't feel it, Raiden, the pull of the darkness. It was all I could do to think, except I couldn't, and I didn't even realise it. There was so much power, and I just wanted more and more, and I couldn't stop. The underworld serenaded me like a siren, the deepest recesses of hell fought to twist me to its whim as I did its inhabitants. If it wasn't for you..." She shook her head, tears escaping from her dark lashes.

"I was fuel to the fire. I gave you a boost, my power melded with yours." He was correct, it did. His power was the only thing that stopped her losing control. She had felt stronger for him, but also anchored.

"But you anchored me, kept me present when everything else tried to rip me away. No matter what it takes, I'll get you out of this, Raiden."

"Maya," he began, but she held up her hand, silencing him.

"No, the things you have done in the past don't matter. I'll offer myself without protest for a full pardon for you. If I have anything to bargain with, that is. I'm sure there are some undead here. It could make detaining me tricky, right? Especially since I don't need to be near any to call for spirits. I can bargain for your freedom with that, right? With my cooperation?"

"Maya, you don't need to bargain for me. Remember I told you there were things I couldn't tell you, well, I can now, and I need you to listen.

"It's true I worked for the Thorne family, but I was never actually theirs. I was removed from basic training at nineteen after I put in my application for the P.T.F. training program. For the last nine years, I've been undercover, feeding them information about the crime families.

That's the reason I had that document on my phone. I saved it on a secure server so, if I ever needed to, I had evidence to prove what I was doing.

"I should have reported it the moment I found the living corpse. I was going to, but then I tracked it to you, and I couldn't do it. But that's not my biggest secret. The truth is, the reason we met was no accident. The family had blackmailed your father into being their surgeon, but as his illness surfaced, he started to get cold feet. They'd always used you as collateral, but they wanted someone present in your life, a constant threat."

"You used me to force my father?"

"It wasn't like that. He'd already agreed, he'd been helping them for years. When I was placed on the scene, the P.T.F. offered him a deal. They knew what he was doing, and in exchange for looking the other way to any of his off-the-books surgeries, he was to become my handler.

"It was getting harder for me to meet with people without raising suspicion. They thought we could use the Thorne family's plan against them. So long as we were together, I could use being with you as a cover for giving information to him, and he in turned passed it on. But the moment I spoke to you was my undoing. You deserved better than being in my world, and yet I couldn't bring myself to let you go.

"When your father died, there was a war brewing between families, you were in real danger. That's when I purged you from their mind, and me from everyone in my old life. I left you for last because I couldn't bear to say goodbye. Just like I couldn't bear to make sure it had worked, the thought of you looking at me and not knowing me, that the eyes that had once adored me would look on me with indifference, it was one step too far."

Maya took a deep breath, closing her eyes as she let the information wash over her. They had met as part of a scheme, but what they had was real. There was no denying that. He had removed himself from their lives to protect her; he had shielded her and her father. She opened her eyes to see him watching her with fierce intensity, searching her face as if it would reveal her thoughts. Did he really expect her to be angry? Another thought crossed her mind.

"Wait. If you're P.T.F., what are you doing in here with me?" She raised her arms, gesturing to their small holding cell.

"I needed you to hear me out. I thought it would go better on this side of the bars." She let her head fall back against the wall with a sigh.

"You look relieved. I thought you'd be angry." His brows furrowed as if trying to make sense of her reaction. The thought made her chuckle. He had removed everyone he had ever met from his life to protect her, and yet he couldn't understand why she wasn't mad.

"Of course I'm relieved. I was scared to death I was going to condemn you right along with me."

"That's what you're worried about? What about you?" He moved to sit beside her again, mirroring her posture to stare at the ceiling, his hand on hers.

"I don't belong in this world. I've seen enough movies to know they were evil. Hell, I raised my own personal army of undead thinking I was saving them. I'm a necromancer, all this time I thought I was healing people and—" She frowned as she heard Raiden begin to laugh. "What?"

"Sorry," he wheezed between laughs, struggling to pull a breath in as he clutched his sides. She levelled a glare towards him, which only made him laugh more, his mirth pausing briefly to be punctuated by an almost choking inhalation, a sound somewhere between humour and pain.

She could see him fighting, trying to stop

himself from laughing, and failing miserably. "It's just," he gasped, dissolving into more laughter. Watching him fight to suppress it caused her own smile to emerge. It was like listening to music, she could listen to that sound forever. "You're a great healer, it's just your timing is sometimes a little off, that's all," he managed to say between breaths.

Her own laugher bubbled up from within as she joined his fitful laughter, tears streaming down her face. It felt good to laugh with him. She didn't remember the last time she had laughed this hard or this long, and for a moment she forgot everything else, her troubles melted away. She leaned against him, noticing his slight wince as he raised his arm to pull her close.

After a while their laughter died, leaving their throats raw and their cheeks stained with tears. She tucked herself closer into his embrace, lifting her feet onto the bed to curl into him as she took a small sip of the water.

"What will they do with me?" she asked seriously, knowing it was time to address the issue at hand.

"Maya, they know what happened at the cemetery was... extenuating circumstances. There was a similar occurrence several months ago when another Perennial awoke."

"Another necromancer?"

"Reaper, and no, she was a phoenix." He wondered why he had corrected her. Why in that moment had making the distinction been important, but there was another word in that sentence that sprung out at her, a more important one.

"Was?"

"Is, I mean is. Perennials are a protected species, although the line for reapers is blurred. Even if you did help locate one of the key members of the Thorne family and uncover one of their underground lairs, there will be consequences, and I have no idea what these will be."

"How do you know this?" This information seemed to come from nowhere, how was it possible he was suddenly updated on the Perennials when no one had been given the time to tell him? Her body told her she hadn't been asleep long, if for no other reason than, when she woke up, she was still wearing the same clothes and her bladder wasn't ready to burst.

"The dart they hit you with put you into hibernation. You've been out for three days, during which time I was debriefed. I asked to be here when you woke. We're alone because they weren't sure exactly what would be waking."

Maya glanced around, noticing for the first time the absolute silence from beyond the prison bars. "Reapers walk a fine line between life and death. They were thought to be a child of the Erinyes, the goddesses of vengeance.

"As such, sometimes they become judge, jury, and executioner for the dead, but sometimes they touch something darker, lose themselves to the powers of the underworld and become its servant, bringing its kingdom to mortal soils. You were different the first time you brought those people back from the dead. It exhausted you because it came from a place of love, of giving. Back in the cemetery, your actions were fuelled by anger and fear, so you touched something darker, and it fed you."

"How do you know there's a difference? You said nothing was known about reapers." She thought back to the people on his list, to how fatigued she had been afterwards and how different their resurrections had felt compared to the thrill of energy that had raced through her.

"There's very little, but I'm telling you what I saw, what I felt. It was different Maya, what you did when you were a medic and what you did back there. It was different. I felt it." She wasn't sure whether he was reinforcing it for his benefit or hers.

"So what happens to me now?"

"Right now, you should let me hold you. Anything else, we will address when the time comes. But I promise you, Maya, whatever happens, I'll be right beside you. My biggest regret is the time I wasted, time when we could have been together."

"You said my father was your handler, do you think he knew about me?" she asked after a prolonged silence.

"I honestly don't know. I think maybe he had his suspicions you were something glorious. I remember during one of our talks he expressed how glad he was you went into surgery. When I asked why I thought he was going to say because he could pass on his mantle, but what he actually said was, 'surgeons know when to step away.' It was the only time he had mentioned it. It wasn't long after that he started to deteriorate.

"He would talk about how relieved he was that you hadn't been born into the Hematophagy Clan like himself. Your birth mother, the breeder, was human, your father never understood how your genes had become abnormal, but he said science and medicine was full of anomalies, just like the one that made him..." He trailed off, but she already knew what he was going to say. Just like the one that made him ill.

"So who became your handler after?" she asked, swallowing.

"Lewis."

"Don't tell me he's P.T.F. too?"

"No, he's family. People underestimate small business owners. He could move a lot more freely than I could. It made feeding information to my contact, Roger, easier. It was a little unorthodox, but since I was living in the flat above him, and could vouch for his character, he acted as an intermediary. Any more questions?" The warmth of his lips on her temple complimented the soothing sensation of his fingers as he traced them across the bare flesh of her arm. It was then she noticed the streaks of mud that should have marred her flesh had been cleaned and her stitches had been removed, leaving a faint white scar where the bullet had grazed her.

"Was my father murdered?" His illness had always bothered her. Those of the Hematophagy Clan didn't suffer diseases. Some, like the vampires, had extended lives, but mainly the other species withing the clan lived a fulfilling life. Even with bad blood, they rarely got sick.

Yet her father's illness not only progressed slowly, it took away the career he loved.

She'd cursed the disease, cursed how it had slowly eaten away at him. She had thought it vindictive, and maybe she'd been right. Even if he was ill, blood should have healed him. Instead, he just grew weaker. No one could explain it, and until now, she'd never had the courage to ask.

"Ask him." He shrugged.

"You did *not* just say that," she scolded, pulling away from him playfully. She froze for a moment, her lips parting as she realised he had been serious. "How would I even do that?"

"How have you done anything? Instinct. Although you'll probably need to learn control first, you wouldn't want to unleash all hell just to get answers to one question."

"I think I'm better off not knowing." But part of her knew that wasn't true, part of her knew she needed to know.

A few hours after Maya had awoken, four armed guards escorted them from the holding area to another remote location. The initial plan seemed to have been to sedate her for transport, but

Raiden's words seemed to hold some weight, and they had agreed to let her walk. It was unnerving how quiet everywhere was. Like the holding cell, aside from those who walked beside her—with their weapons pointed towards her with fingers on the triggers—she didn't see a single soul.

She hadn't understood why she had been moved, but it had been impossible not to notice the sheer quantity of pine trees that surrounded the modest dwelling. At first she marvelled at the wild herb garden which grew below the wooden porch and thought the dill wreath above the doors had been a beautifully decorative touch.

It was only when Raiden told her the cabin was made from hazel, because it was thought to keep evil spirits away, their relocation made more sense, as did the scent of sage, and the hanging sprigs of holly she could see twisting in the breeze from the barely opened barred windows.

Despite being a wooden cabin, the security system was state of the art. The moment they crossed the threshold, the door had locked. On the outside, beside the door, was a control panel, similar to those used at the hospital, and she didn't even need to try it to know she did not possess the authorisation to open the door.

The glass of the barred windows was

reinforced, and with the drapes drawn back, the lacquered wooden flooring created a constant reminder of the prison she was in. The sawdust and wood shavings suggested the bars were a new feature, and as if having bars mounted on both the inside and outside hadn't been enough, when she pushed her hand through to try to open the window further to enjoy the scents of the forest and fragrant herb garden, she found they could only be pushed up those first few inches before the locking mechanisms kicked in.

Despite the cabin being comfortable and possessing all the conveniences she could need, there was no question in her mind that it was still a prison, and the combination of the hanging charms and fresh etchings on the walls, which had yet to dull with dust and time, told her it was a prison that had been modified specifically for her.

They believed her to be as dangerous as she felt, and she couldn't blame them. The consideration had been nice, allowing her to spend her final days in comfort with Raiden beside her, instead of trapped in a small cell with nothing but the ticking of a clock to count down her remaining time.

The door opened straight into an open-plan lounge, kitchen, diner. With half of the upstairs left open, the room enjoyed the natural lighting from the skylights and an airy feel. Upstairs was a single bedroom with en-suite bathroom and a large storage space that Maya thought would be put to better use as a study. On the ground floor were two more bedrooms, and a large bathroom. It didn't feel like a prison, it felt like a home. It had been furnished with simple items, and while it looked as if it had been lived in, it was devoid of any personal touches.

The only information she had managed to ascertain was this was the place they were to wait for sentencing. Even with all the precautions for warding away evil, Maya wasn't sure it would make any real difference if she tried to connect to her power again, but she had no intention of trying. She was determined to make the most of her remaining days, and she was certain that was precisely what these were.

Even with his injuries, Raiden had done everything within his power to keep her mind off the looming sentence. He spoke freely about his time in the training academy, how it had always been his intention to apply for the P.T.F. training program, and how instead of accepting him they had pulled him from his military school, arranging for it to appear he had been expelled and arrested for his violent temperament and the discovery of years' worth of sabotage and data manipulation on the academy systems.

He had been thrown into a cell with Zaz, a newly recruited appraiser taken under the wing of the Thorne family. They had told him just what to say. His story and gifts were so compelling that when Zaz was released, he had told the family everything about his recent discovery. About the young man who could manipulate ice and lightning and could use his electrical alignment to create untraceable, sentient computer viruses to purge information from any storage system.

It was his ability to do this that had made Raiden realise he could also erase memories. After all, the brain was nothing more than a sophisticated computer.

He had only been in prison for a few months when they had taken the bait. Suddenly new evidence was found that saw him acquitted of all charges. On the day of his release, they had been waiting for him with a car, and news of a debt not only for freeing him from prison, but to settle the outstanding loan his parents had taken out before their deaths.

From that day forth, he rose in their ranks, completing hits on other gang members and arranging witness protection where needed when civilian targets had to disappear. The only things he had done beyond the P.T.F.'s scope had been the disposal of those Maya had risen.

He had documented each case, and whilst he would be disciplined for his actions, his superiors had shown leniency due to the results. Luiza had been charged as Pyre-starter when damning evidence came to light in a closed-door trial, and as far as the public were concerned, the threat was over.

Three days passed in a blur as they talked, laughed, and enjoyed each other as if trying to recapture the missing years. But with each setting of the sun, Maya found it more difficult to keep her mind from her own trial. She knew she wouldn't be allowed to attend. The camera on her belt was the only evidence they needed.

Raiden sat behind her on the sofa, his body pressed against her as she leaned back into him, enjoying the featherlight touch of his fingers through her hair as they talked and laughed together. She felt her smile fade as she heard a loud knock, quickly followed by the lock disengaging. She froze, forgetting to breathe, as Raiden stood, wrestling his way from behind her to stand beside her wearing the same weighted expression. His lips lifted in a reassuring smile he couldn't maintain as he watched the door in apprehension.

"I'll get drinks," Raiden whispered, no doubt intending to give her some privacy. She grasped his wrist, silently begging him to stay.

As a figure entered, Maya blinked a few times, her mind at war with itself trying to determine what this man looked like, if his hair was dark or pale, his eyes blue or brown, if he was tall, or short. Just looking at him made her eyes hurt and her temples throb. She squeezed her eyes closed, opening them again, but it didn't help.

"Give it a second, my glamour doesn't seem to work so well on you Perennials." He stood by the open door as if he thought the natural lighting would somehow help until, eventually, her mind settled on him having dark blond hair, brown eyes and features so sharp they had to have been etched with a chisel.

"Glamour?" she questioned, tilting her head, waiting to see if his image would alter again.

"Yes, knowledge I assume will not leave this room." Maya nodded, not daring to ask any more questions. "Sorry to have kept you waiting. I am P.T.F. Alpha Alex Ciele."

Maya stiffened, leaning into the touch she felt slide over her shoulders. She placed one of her hands to Raiden's, holding him in place, needing the comfort of his touch, unsure when his wrist had slipped from her grasp. This was it. She was going to discover when and how her sentence would be carried out.

"I was hoping we could talk." The door closed behind him, but not before she saw the silhouettes of some other people waiting outside. Executioners, she thought. They weren't going to waste any time with further delays. She'd been handed a death sentence. Raiden's grasp tightened in response to her slightest tremble.

"How long do I have to put my affairs in order?"

"A few days. Would that be acceptable? Although I will need an answer before I leave?"

"I'd like it to be quick. Quick and private." She glanced over her shoulder at Raiden, part of her wondering if she was wrong stopping him from leaving, for making him endure this. Her insides churned tumultuously as she stared at Alex, her eyes unable to release her executioner from their sights.

"I'm sorry, I'm not following." He perched himself on the arm of the sofa furthest from her, looking oddly relaxed for someone delivering a death sentence. His gaze levelled at her. For a moment, his eyes seemed to alter in shade before becoming brown again.

"I know I made a mistake, but if it could be done behind closed doors... I don't think I could handle a public execution." There, she'd spoken the words. There was no need to drag this out any longer than necessary.

"Execution?"

"Yes, aren't you..."

"Has no one come by to talk to you?" Alex placed his fingers to his brow, taking a slow breath. "Of course not," he whispered on a sigh. "Let's start again. Your sentence was announced a few days ago, but we have to discuss terms first. The P.T.F. would like to enlist your skills for a period of no less than five years, both as a surgeon and Perennial in exchange for all charges being dropped. Is that acceptable?"

She wasn't sure what her expression must have looked like, but she didn't miss the way the corners of his lips twitched as if he was holding back a smile. Her grasp tightened on Raiden's hand. Barely able to believe what she had heard, she glanced to him as if confirming her ears weren't party to some deception. His expression gave the only answer she needed to hear.

"What? Yes, I mean..." She tried to breathe through the relief but saw dark motes appear in her gaze. She dipped her head, focusing on the floor as she pulled in breath after breath until she saw the small droplets pooling at her feet from her silent tears.

Raiden was rubbing her back, talking softly, his words lost through the roaring of blood in her ears. This seemed too good to be true. There had to be a catch, but if that catch meant she got to live, she got to spend more time with the love of her life, then she would give them anything they wanted. Even if it meant being a lab-rat. She could endure anything so long as she was able to fall into Raiden's arms at the end of the day.

"Then let me introduce you to your team." Raiden slid around the sofa, perching himself on the chair arm next to her, wrapping his arm around her shoulder to calm her tears. She hadn't realised how tense she had been about the verdict until it had been delivered. How much she had actually wanted to live. She couldn't believe she was being given another chance. Alex hovered at the door, waiting for her to compose herself before inviting in the people who had been waiting outside with an incline of his head.

"Firstly, my sister, Ashley Ciele, and next to her is Jesse Kyron." The two figures from outside entered. Ashley, the woman with beautiful rust-coloured locks and eyes the colour of grey satin, smiled brightly at her while Jesse, the other woman with the blonde hair and blue eyes, waved an awkward greeting as they were encouraged inside. "Both are Perennials like yourself. Along with their partners, they are our newest task force. One geared towards quelling the uprising against the current council of elders.

"Like yourself, both of these fine women have connected with their soul mates, meaning their already formidable powers are boosted by their presence. We can arrange for you to meet them at a later date, but I would like the three of you to spend a little time together this evening so they can tell you what to expect."

"Soul mates?" She saw Alex's skin flush slightly before she turned her vision to Raiden.

"I had some amends to make before forcing that revelation on her," Raiden muttered, kissing the crown of her head. Maya swallowed. Soul mates. She couldn't think of a more perfect term for what the two of them shared. Her gaze returned to the two women, the one called Ashley had already claimed the large armchair for her own, while Jess seemed to be content standing, leaning against the hearth.

"So what is going to happen to me now?"

"You're going to be staying here as part of our

surgical team, and you're going to learn how to use your reaper abilities in a controlled and disciplined manner," Alex revealed.

"I don't think that's a good idea, it's too dark." Maya shook her head slowly, fear bubbling up within her. She had evaded a death sentence, but to touch on such forces again was unthinkable. They couldn't seriously be wanting her to learn to harness something so dark, so evil. She had barely survived intact last time. What if Raiden wasn't there to anchor her, what if he couldn't reach her? It was too much, too powerful, too dark.

"Yes, and Raiden is your light. He will both empower and ground you like he did in the cemetery. He will protect your soul because it belongs to him. No one else could stop you falling, but it will still be difficult. I'll be honest, in case you haven't already realised" —he gestured to the room around him at the charms and precautions— "people are afraid of your skills. It'll be difficult to win them over, especially while showing them what you can do."

"Can I not just act as your surgeon, and maybe get a suppressor?" That was the better option, the safer option for everyone.

"Suppressors don't work on us." Ashley moved to sit on the sofa beside her, placing a reassuring hand on Maya's knee. "We have talked about things a lot over the last two days, and along with Raiden, you'll be working closely with Conrad, my soul-mate. He's an ifrit, as such he's attuned to the underworld. He should be able to sense when things become too much. It's going to be scary at first, but we've got you. You're one of us now, you'll find no judgement with us. We'll help you embrace and understand this part of you safely." Maya wanted to hug Ashley, her tone, the encouraging touches, all of it eased the pressure in her chest, made her feel almost as if things could be alright.

"I don't think safe and necromancy fall into the same reality," Maya whispered. She closed her eyes, taking comfort in the gentle pressure of Raiden's touch. The notion of willingly delving back into that world terrified her, but with him beside her, she was sure she could face anything. "Okay," she whispered shakily, nodding her head. Bless her heart, the young woman beside her gave her such a winning smile. Maya found herself grinning back.

"Then welcome aboard, Maya." Alex expended his hand, with only the slightest hesitation Maya accepted, praying she had not just made the worst mistake of her life.

Dear reader,

We hope you enjoyed reading *Rekindled Sparks*. Please take a moment to leave a review, even if it's a short one. Your opinion is important to us.

Discover more books by Kathryn Jayne at https://www.nextchapter.pub/authors/kathryn-jayne

Want to know when one of our books is free or discounted? Join the newsletter at http://eepurl.com/bqqB3H

Best regards,

Kathryn Jayne and the Next Chapter Team